Cole Yearned To Touch Lucky.

He wanted to run his hands down her womanly hips and pull her to him. He could almost feel her soft, sweet body pressing against him.

"Lucky?"

She stood in the doorway with towels, a washcloth and an unwrapped bar of soap in her hands. She knew she shouldn't be staring at him, inspecting every inch of his broad, hairy chest, but her eyes refused to give up the pleasure. She'd been around men all her life, but never had the sight of a man's naked chest taken her breath away. Her fingers itched to touch him, to glide through the thicket of black hair that covered Cole Kendrick from neck to waist.

"I...I... Here's the towels and soap." Lucky lay the items on a table near the door.

"Lucky?"

No, no, her mind screamed. Don't answer that invitation you see in his eyes, that you feel emanating from his body. "Good night, Mr. Kendrick," she said, then turned and ran.

Dear Reader:

Sensuous, emotional, compelling...these are all words that describe Silhouette Desire. If this is your first Desire novel, let me extend an invitation for you to sit back, kick off your shoes and revel in the pleasure of a tantalizing, fulfilling love story. If you're a regular reader, you already know that you're in for a real treat!

A Silhouette Desire can encompass many varying moods and tones. The story can be deeply moving and dramatic, or charming and lighthearted. But no matter what, each and every Silhouette Desire is a terrific romance written by and for today's woman.

I know you'll love March's *Man of the Month* book, *McAllister's Lady* by Naomi Horton. Also, look for *Granite Man*, one of Elizabeth Lowell's WESTERN LOVERS series. And don't miss wonderful love stories by some undeniable favorites *and* exciting newcomers: Kelly Jamison, Lucy Gordon, Beverly Barton and Karen Leabo.

So give in to Desire...you'll be glad you did!

All the best,

Lucia Macro
Senior Editor

BEVERLY BARTON

LUCKY IN LOVE

SILHOUETTE *Desire*®

Published by Silhouette Books New York

America's Publisher of Contemporary Romance

SILHOUETTE BOOKS
300 East 42nd St., New York, N.Y. 10017

LUCKY IN LOVE

Copyright © 1991 by Beverly Beaver

ISBN: 0-373-05628-1

First Silhouette Books printing March 1991

Printed in the U.S.A.

BEVERLY BARTON

has been in love with romance since her grandfather gave her an illustrated book of *Beauty and the Beast*. An avid reader since childhood, she began writing at the age of nine and wrote short stories, poetry, plays and novels throughout high school and college. After marriage to her own "hero" and the births of her daughter and son, she chose to be a full-time home-maker, a.k.a. wife, mother, friend and volunteer.

Six years ago, she began substitute teaching and returned to writing as a hobby. In 1987 she joined the RWA and soon afterward helped found the Heart of Dixie chapter in Alabama. Her hobby became an obsession as she devoted more and more time to improving her skills as a writer. Now, her lifelong dream of becoming published has come true.

To my first fan,
who read all my immature scribblings,
Nancy Sue Elkins
Cousin by chance, dearest friend by choice.
Special thanks to
my son Brant for "technical advice"
and
my fellow Heart of Dixie Romance Writers
for loving support and encouragement.

One

Lucky Darnell looked across the kitchen table at the elderly man whose keen eyes gave away nothing as he studied the cards in his hand.

Was he bluffing? she wondered. Well, there was only one way to find out. "I'll see your hundred and raise you two hundred." She pushed six rolls of pennies toward the large center pile of coins.

Suddenly a loud boom of thunder shook the house, startling the four people gathered in Lucky's big, old-fashioned kitchen. A flash of lightning followed, its frightening brilliance setting the windowpanes ablaze.

Lucky gasped involuntarily, then groaned when unexpected darkness claimed the room.

"Oh, Lord, that scared me to death," a teenage female voice said.

"It's our damn antiquated utility department. Every little rain cloud causes a power outage," Pudge Prater said, and though Lucky couldn't see a thing, she could easily imagine him contorting his thin lips into a grimace, deepening the tiny wrinkles lining his fat face from bald head to double chin.

Lucky felt movement at her side and heard a peculiar rustling sound. "Uncle Pudge, what are you doing?"

Just as abruptly as they had gone off, the lights came on. Lucky looked immediately to her eighty-year-old great-uncle, who stared directly back at her and smiled.

"Full house," the old man said, laying his cards faceup on the wooden table.

"You cheated, you old reprobate." Lucky threw her cards on the table and jumped to her feet, placing her hands on her hips.

"How could I have cheated?" he asked innocently, a devilish twinkle in his warm hazel eyes. "The lights were out. I couldn't see a thing."

Lucky knew the other two card players wouldn't say a word while they watched Uncle Pudge and her reenact a scene that was the highlight of their weekly poker games. Rich was an old friend accustomed to her temperament and Pudge's affinity for cheating. And Rich's teenage daughter, Suzy, merely smothered a giggle when Lucky scooped up a handful of rolled pennies. "All bets are off. You cheated. I don't know how, but you did. Rich and Suzy know it as well as I do."

"Now, Lucky Lu, just cool that redheaded temper of yours and—"

A rumble of distant thunder echoed. A current of white light illuminated the black October sky, and total darkness enveloped the room once again.

"Oh, no," Suzy said.

"Everybody stay calm. I'll go get a kerosene lamp." Lucky laid the rolled coins on the table and slowly made her way across the kitchen, her hands outstretched to help her feel her way to the door.

When she reached the dining room, a lightning streak revealed a clear path to the entrance hall. Quickly she dashed across the oak floors, her yellow jogging shoes making silent contact.

Why hadn't she left the lamp on the screened back porch where Granny had always kept it? Because you thought it would look good on the cherry table in the foyer, she scolded herself. And of course her flashlight was in the glove compartment of her car. Hindsight was wonderful, Lucky decided as she walked down the entrance hall.

When she neared the cherry table, Lucky felt a gush of cool air surround her, and pinpricks of rain hit her face. Someone must have left the front door open, she thought, reaching out in the darkness.

Her hand touched something solid. Her fingers explored, discovering a soft fuzziness covering a hard surface. Tentatively she moved her hand upward. Just as she touched what she recognized as human flesh, splintering light shot from heaven to earth, spotlighting the handsome devil standing in her doorway. A scream froze in her throat as her mouth opened in a silent cry.

In that split second, she'd seen a tall, muscular man whose dark eyes mirrored her own shock. Her bewildered mind tried to rationalize. Who was this gorgeous man? What was he doing standing in her open front door? Why couldn't she scream or speak or move?

Realizing her fingers were still on his face, Lucky jerked her hand away, cleared her throat and tried to talk.

"Who...who..." Get hold of yourself, she thought. Think. Think. She wasn't alone in the house. She could call for help.

"May I come in out of the rain?" the intruder asked in a husky voice filled with irritation.

Before she could reply, the stranger stepped inside, and
his rather formidable body collided with hers. "Sorry," he
said. "I can't see a thing. I thought you'd moved out of the
way."

Lucky trembled when she felt the cool dampness of his
chest soak into her blouse. As if realizing how his unexpected appearance might have unnerved her, he clamped
his fingers about her shoulders in gentle reassurance. The
scent of wet male and light woodsy cologne emanated from
his big, virile body.

"Ms. Darnell's expecting me tomorrow." His hands
continued holding her, keeping their bodies in intimate
contact. "I'm Cole Kendrick."

Lucky's breath caught in her lungs. This wasn't supposed to happen, she thought. *I've seen his picture in the
paper, seen him on TV. I don't like baseball. I'm not impressed by celebrity athletes.* When Don had called about
letting the great Mr. Kendrick stay here at Holly House for
a recuperative period, she was certain she'd be immune to
the irresistible charms that had other women falling at his
feet. But here she was practically speechless, her heart
hammering with excitement and her body tingling with
anticipation. No, no. That can't be true, she assured herself. *He scared the living daylights out of me. That's why
I'm having this peculiar reaction to him.*

Lucky pulled away, taking several cautious steps backward. "Ah, I . . . I'm Lucky Darnell. You've arrived at a
bad time, Mr. Kendrick. I came out here to get a lamp. It's
over on the table. This storm seems to have knocked out
our power. I . . . we didn't hear you knock. Of course, the
thunder was so loud."

She knew she was babbling, but couldn't seem to stop
herself. This man made her nervous, and that nervous-
ness had very little to do with fear and a great deal to do
with her female hormones having gone into overdrive.

"I've got a lighter in my pocket. If you can find the lamp, maybe we can—"

Lucky grappled in the dark, seeking the stranger's hand with the intention of leading him toward the cherry table. Her fingers missed their mark, grazing the side of his lean hip. She groaned inwardly, feeling a sense of embarrassment. The instant she touched him, Cole stiffened, reached out and grabbed her hand.

"Lucky!" Uncle Pudge's gravelly voice called from the kitchen. "What's going on in there, gal? Did you get lost and start talking to yourself?"

"My great-uncle," she told her visitor. "We had a card game going on when the lights went out."

She found the small Queen Anne table, dropped Cole's hand, clasped the glass lamp and held it out in front of her. "I'm all right," she told her uncle. "I've got the lamp." Then to Cole she said, "I'll take off the chimney. You light the wick."

Lucky heard a faint click. A tiny flame flickered in Cole Kendrick's hand, dispersing a mellow glow within its limited range. She wanted to look at him, but refrained from raising her eyes upward. For several seconds she gazed at his broad hand, noticing the sprinkling of black hair across the top and the long, well-shaped fingers.

"Are you going to light this thing?" His voice startled her, making her hand shake and her gaze move to his face.

"Yes, of course." When she removed the chimney, Cole set the fire to the wick, and warm, golden light filled the hallway.

He flipped the lid on the lighter, returned it to his pocket and placed both hands over Lucky's where they held the base of the kerosene lamp.

"You're trembling." He looked into her eyes and smiled. "I'm sorry if I frightened you. I should have called and told you that I was leaving a day early."

Lucky stared at him, her heart pounding loudly in her ears. He looked big, tough and powerful, even with his mouth curled into a smile and his wet sable hair plastered to his forehead.

"It's all right. There wouldn't have been a problem if the power hadn't gone out."

She couldn't stop looking at him, memorizing every line of his ruggedly handsome face. She found the drops of moisture clinging to his high cheekbones fascinating, and had a sudden urge to lick them away. This is ridiculous, she thought. *I'm acting like an idiot.*

"Does that happen often?"

"What? Oh . . . no, not really. Despite what my uncle thinks, the power's off because of the storm."

"It's pretty rough out there. The wind's started up."

Lucky wondered if he thought it odd that he was standing, soaking wet, in the foyer of an antebellum house, holding an antique lamp between himself and a stranger. By the look in his compelling brown eyes, she suspected he was under the same hypnotic spell as she.

"Wow!" Suzy Brewster's gangly young body stopped dead still in the dining-room doorway as she gaped at Lucky and Cole. "Cole Kendrick right here in Florence, Alabama, standing in my friend Lucky's foyer. Wow!"

Surprised, the couple turned toward the voice that interrupted their private interlude. Under normal circumstances, Lucky adored Suzy and enjoyed her company. After all, her father had been Greg's best friend, and Rich and his daughter always reminded her of the good times she had shared with her husband. But she knew Mr. Kendrick was seeking solitude and anonymity. The last thing he wanted was a teenage fan gushing over him, then spreading the news that a celebrity was in their midst.

"What's he doing here?" Suzy asked exuberantly. "Gosh, Lucky, I didn't know you knew Cole Kendrick."

Lucky felt Cole's hands tense before he removed them from hers. "Mr. Kendrick is going to be renting a room here at Holly House for a few weeks. But I don't want you to tell anyone. He's come here for some peace and quiet. Do you understand?"

"Gee. Yeah, I guess so."

Cole walked over to Suzy and offered his hand. "Hi, Suzy. I'm always glad to meet a fan." Man and girl exchanged smiles and friendly handshakes.

"Just think, Lucky," Suzy said, gazing at the hand that had just touched her idol's, "when you open Holly House as a bed and breakfast next spring, you can advertise that Cole Kendrick was your first guest."

"I'll have a sign painted, saying Cole Kendrick Slept Here, and hang it outside." The moment the words were out of her mouth, she wished them back. She felt his eyes on her, inviting her to look at him. She did, and regretted the impulsive act. Humor etched the lines of his strongly masculine face, and something almost like a dare glinted in his dark eyes. It's as if he's hinting that his nights here won't be spent sleeping alone, she thought.

"Great idea. Hey, come on in the kitchen and meet my dad. Oh, and Uncle Pudge. He's going to pass out. He's as big a fan as I am. He even had to buy a portable TV just so he and Lucky wouldn't fight during baseball season," the girl said.

Suzy grabbed Cole's hand and pulled him into the dining room. Lucky noticed that he walked with a slight limp, and the knowledge that his accident had left him with a permanent reminder made her want to comfort him. This man was a stranger. He meant nothing to her, yet she felt drawn to him in a way she couldn't explain, even to herself.

Cole turned to look back at Lucky, who followed a few steps behind, walking slowly as she gripped their only source of light in her hand. "Aren't you a baseball lover, Ms. Darnell?"

Cole followed Suzy while a stunned Lucky hesitated at the kitchen doorway, uncertain how to answer his question. Why had he said "lover" instead of "fan"? she wondered. Exactly what was he asking? She knew she had to stop overreacting to everything the man said, or she'd be a basket case by the time he went back to Memphis.

Suzy didn't wait for Lucky to reply. "The only sports she likes are fishing and poker. As for baseball, she'd rather watch orchestras playing and ballet dancers twirling. That's why Uncle Pudge got his own TV."

"Baseball too lowbrow for you, or are you one of those women who don't like to see grown men playing... hitting balls... sweating... scoring?"

Lucky swallowed, hoping to dislodge the lump in her throat and recover her powers of speech. He kept catching her off guard. She simply wasn't used to men like Cole Kendrick, men who were brutally male and accustomed to taking what they wanted. He was nothing like the Southern gentlemen with whom she'd associated all her life. He was the total opposite of Gregory Darnell, whose boyish charm and courtly manners had captivated her from the moment they'd met during her freshman year in college.

"I have nothing against sports, Mr Kendrick. I simply believe in the old adage 'to each his own.'"

Suzy practically dragged Cole into the kitchen, her enthusiasm obvious to everyone. "Look who I've got. Can you believe it?"

"So this was what was taking Lucky so long." Pudge Prater eyed his great-niece as he stood up to shake Cole's hand. "Decided to come on early, huh? Well, we're damn glad to have you here, boy."

"This is my great-uncle, Jefferson Davis Prater, and that's Suzy's father, Dr. Richard Brewster. I don't suppose I need to introduce Mr. Kendrick to either of you,'' Lucky said.

"How come nobody told me he was coming?" Suzy continued clinging to Cole's hand.

"Because, Miss Big Mouth, you can't keep a secret," Rich said, casting a fake frown in his daughter's direction. Father and child shared a striking resemblance, both tall and slender with pale blue eyes and raven black hair. "I assure you, sir, that this young lady won't impose on you or tell any of her friends that you're here."

"Thanks, Dr. Brewster. I appreciate that." Cole wiped the lingering moisture from his face. "I'm afraid I'm ruining the floor, Ms. Darnell."

"Don't give it a thought, my boy," Pudge said, patting Cole on the shoulder. "It'll mop up. Lucky, see if you can find him a towel or something so he can dry his hair."

Realizing that Uncle Pudge had caught her staring at Cole, Lucky tried to mentally prepare herself for the onslaught of matchmaking that was sure to follow. Since Greg's death four years ago, the old man had been determined to see her happily remarried. She couldn't make him understand that she wasn't sure if that was what she really wanted out of life. Even though her marriage had been a good one, Greg's illness and youthful death had taken its toll on her emotions, leaving her afraid of experiencing such intense pain ever again.

Lucky set the lamp on the counter near the sink and rummaged through a drawer filled with kitchen towels, trying to find the newest one. Rich and Pudge exchanged baseball chitchat with the visiting celebrity while Suzy gazed at him in star-struck adoration.

The hum of electrical energy and the glow from several sixty-watt bulbs instantly caught the attention of everyone in the room.

Lucky pulled a green-checked dish towel from the drawer, purposely avoiding any eye contact with her guest. If she blushed in darkness or lamplight, he wouldn't know, but now there would be no way to hide her emotional reaction to him. Once again she cursed the ivory-pale complexion that exposed her private feelings and burned, unfashionably, instead of tanned in the sunlight.

"How about some hot coffee?" Lucky asked, looking at Rich. "I could put some on now and fix sandwiches. Are you hungry, Mr. Kendrick?" She knew she was doing it again, talking compulsively because she was nervous. "There's cake left from supper, and I could open a bag of chips."

The two men exchanged glances, then Cole turned toward Lucky. "Coffee and sandwiches would be nice."

"Don't fix for us. Suzy and I need to head for home while the rain seems to have slacked off some." Rich removed his corduroy sport coat from the back of the Windsor armchair. "Get your sweater, sweetheart."

"Ah, Daddy, do we have to leave now?" A pouting Suzy picked up her sweater from the small antique sideboard and wrapped it around her shoulders. "Can I come back and see you, Mr. Kendrick? I promise I won't tell a living soul you're here."

"I'll look forward to seeing you again," Cole said, flashing his nationally recognizable smile. "And the name's Cole."

Rich hustled his reluctant daughter out the back door, leaving an amused Pudge Prater looking back and forth from his great-niece to the damp guest standing there in soggy Reeboks.

"Well, children, this tired old man is going to bed," Pudge said none too subtly. "Glad you're here, Cole. I'll see you in the morning."

"Uncle Pudge?" Lucky felt a sudden sense of panic., She didn't want to be left alone with Cole. She took several steps away from the counter at the same moment he walked toward her.

"He didn't hear your call for help." Cole nodded his head in the direction of the empty doorway through which the elderly man had made a hasty exit.

Lucky gritted her teeth, willing her tongue to silence until she could dampen her hot temper. How dare this man assume she was afraid to be alone with him, even if she was. She had never liked overly confident males, and she certainly didn't intend to make an exception with Mr. Tall, Dark and Devastating.

"Could I have the towel to dry my hair?" Cole glanced at the checked cloth clutched tightly in Lucky's hand.

Without saying a word, she tossed the towel, which, to her dismay, he caught in midair.

"Thanks."

"I'll put on the coffee." She told herself that if she didn't look at him, everything would be all right. She began preparing the coffee and sandwiches. "Ham or chicken?" she asked as she stood at the open refrigerator.

"You choose. You'll find I'm not a very picky eater." Cole rubbed the towel vigorously over his head one last time, then tossed the cloth across the room. It landed with a dull thud directly in the sink.

Surprised by the flying dish towel, Lucky jerked her head up. Cole Kendrick's arms were crossed at his waist, his big hands pulling at the hem of his blue-and-white argyle sweater. In one quick, sure move, he yanked the sweater up and over his head. He ran his fingers through his still-damp hair, trying without success to straighten the unruly sable strands.

"Is there somewhere I could hang my sweater?" He held the soft diamond-patterned sweater in his hand.

For a few seconds Lucky couldn't take her eyes off his pale blue shirt. It was plastered to his chest, the moisture giving it a translucent quality that revealed a mass of dark chest hair from neck to waist.

"Uh, I . . . lay it on the counter. I'll . . . I'll hang it up later." *This isn't like me,* she thought. *I don't turn into a quivering, tongue-tied female at the sight of an attractive man, not even one who gives new meaning to the word* sexy.

"I think I'll wait till morning to get my suitcase out of the car." Cole sat down at the table, watching Lucky slice large chunks from a huge ham shank. "I'm sorry I didn't call before I left Memphis, but I . . . well, I was eager to get away."

"It's no problem. Really." Lucky sliced a ripe tomato and arranged several slices on top of the ham. "Your room's ready. All I have to do is take up some fresh towels and soap for the upstairs bathroom. It's seldom used, since Uncle Pudge sleeps downstairs and I have a bath adjoining my bedroom."

"I suppose I'm sort of a guinea pig for your new venture, aren't I?"

She glanced at the coffee maker to see if it had finished brewing. "Yes, I guess you are. I hope our arrangement will help us both. It will give me a chance to play hostess for the bed and breakfast I plan to open next spring."

"And if this place gives me the solitude and privacy I need, it will be well worth the double price I've paid."

"When Don called a few weeks ago and asked me to let you come here and stay, I explained what a bad time this was for me. Moving my antique shop from downtown Florence out here to Holly House and preparing for a big pre-Christmas opening won't leave much time to cater to a guest."

"Your cousin told me all that before I mailed you my check. I don't expect you to cater to me. I've had eighteen months of doctors, nurses, specialists of all kinds hovering over me night and day. My own sister nearly drove me crazy."

Lucky poured steaming coffee into a brown earthenware mug. "I can assure you that I'll be far too busy to give you more than a minimum of my time."

"Don told me that this old place has been in your family for generations." Cole looked around the enormous kitchen, taking note of how well the modern appliances blended with fine antiques to give the room an aura of timelessness.

"You and Don must have become pretty good friends for him to discuss the family with you."

Cole readjusted his long frame on the oak chair, rubbing one leg from hip to knee. The doctors had told him that he'd probably walk with a slight limp for the rest of his life. Although the pain would lessen in time, a leg held together with nuts and bolts would forever be a reminder that a drunken driver had ended his major-league baseball career. "Yeah. Don became much more than my physical therapist. His contrary bossiness wouldn't let me give up when I wanted to time and time again."

"That sounds like Don, all right. He always was bossy, even as a kid." Lucky placed the ham sandwich and mug of coffee in front of Cole. "While you eat, I'll run upstairs and make sure everything's ready."

Cole grabbed Lucky's wrist and pulled her toward him. Nervous gray eyes met determined brown ones. "Stay and talk to me while I eat." Cole wasn't sure what it was about this woman that intrigued him so, but she fascinated him in a way no other woman ever had. Perhaps it was the combination of desire and wariness he saw in her eyes every time she looked at him. Her fiery independence

seemed to be at odds with her cultured Southern courtesy
and soft femininity. And God, she smelled good. Womanly. Fresh and flower sweet. Everything about her seemed
to be a contradiction. Maybe that was the attraction, or
maybe he was simply reacting to her like any red-blooded
man would to a beautiful woman.

She hesitated, her insides quivering like warm jelly. She
willed her hand not to tremble, but couldn't stop the flush
of warmth that spread through her body, tautening her
nipples and heating her blood. She couldn't want this man.
She couldn't! He was a stranger, and Lucille Leticia Darnell had never lusted after a man in her life.

Cole tugged on her wrist, pulling her closer and closer
until her legs brushed against his knees. "Whatever you
need to do upstairs can wait, can't it?"

"Yes, I...I suppose it can." Lucky yanked her wrist free
from his hold and stepped back, shoving her nervous
hands into the pockets of her faded jeans.

When she realized that Cole's gaze was riveted to her
hips, she removed her hands and sat down beside him. He
ate several bites from the sandwich, then took several sips
of coffee. "This coffee's great."

"Oh, dear, I forgot to ask if you take cream or sugar.
Uncle Pudge and I both drink ours black, so I—"

"It's fine. Just the way I like it." Cole's big hand encompassed the mug as he brought it to his lips again. "So,
tell me about yourself, your uncle, Holly House and Florence, Alabama."

Lucky laughed, the sound deep and throaty. "That
would take all night, especially filling you in on Uncle
Pudge and Holly House."

"I've got all night."

"Well, I'm afraid I don't. I have a busy day tomorrow."

"Oh. Well, how about telling me something about Lucky Darnell?"

"There's not much to tell. Compared to you, I've lived a very dull life. I was born, raised and educated here in Florence. I married my college sweetheart. We opened our own antique shop on Court Street and were very happy until he died four years ago."

"Did you and your husband live here at Holly House?"

"No, we had an apartment. You see, my grandmother and Uncle Pudge lived here alone until her death last year. As with many old Southern families, ours didn't have the money to keep this place maintained the way it should have been. Now it's going to take thousands and thousands of dollars to restore it."

"Is that why you're planning on turning it into a bed and breakfast next year?"

"Yes. I'm hoping that between my antique shop and the bed and breakfast, I'll be able to eventually make all the improvements needed." She wanted to tell him that there was more to her problems than simply restoring her family's homestead, but knew she had no business pouring her heart out to a man who'd be gone in a few weeks.

"Your life doesn't sound at all dull to me, Ms. Darnell, compared to mine or anyone else's. At least you've been allowed to live your life without every action making headlines."

"Don told me the reporters hounded you even while you were in the hospital and that women would disguise themselves as nurses in order to sneak into your room."

When her cousin had told her about those adoring fans, she couldn't imagine why grown women would act so foolishly. But sitting across from Cole, her heart beating erratically and her palms damp with perspiration, she realized the effect he had on the female of the species.

Cole swallowed the last drops from his mug. "Despite what the newspapers print, I'm not a womanizer. Oh, I sowed some wild oats when I was younger, but in the past seven or eight years, my tastes have become very discriminating."

"Your love life is really none of my business." She knew she couldn't allow herself to become involved with this man. The last thing she needed was a brief affair and a broken heart.

"I'm making it your business." When Cole reached across the table for Lucky's hand, she snatched it away and stood up.

"It's getting late, Mr. Kendrick. I'd like to show you to your room now so I can go to bed. I have to get up early tomorrow."

Cole stood beside her, his muscular arm brushing against her slender one. "Lead the way," he said, barely suppressing a chuckle.

"We'll go up the back stairs. I've prepared the first bedroom on the left for you. It's the one closest to the bath."

As they made their way out into the hallway and up the back staircase, Lucky wished she'd never agreed to let this man come to Holly House, even as a favor to Don.

"Here we are," she said as she walked into the spacious room and flipped on the wall switch. Light from the brass chandelier spread a creamy transparent veil over every inch of the elegant old room. "Make yourself at home. I'll get the towels and soap. You might want to take a hot shower before going to bed."

"Yes, I'd like that. Thank you." Cole watched as she hurried past him and out the door. He knew that on some level Lucky Darnell was afraid of him, and he didn't want her to be. He wanted the beautiful redhead to like him. He wasn't sure why, but it was important to him that they become friends. Some gut instinct told him that they needed each other.

Cole glanced around the room and was immediately drawn to the inviting four-poster bed. The covers had been turned down, revealing ivory cotton sheets, and a colorful quilt lay folded at the foot. He wasn't too familiar with furniture styles, modern or antique, but he recognized a pair of Chippendale chairs. They were almost identical to the ones in Kristin's bedroom, and he remembered that she'd taken great delight in telling him just how much she'd paid for them. If there was one thing his ex-fiancée knew, it was the going price of things.

Damn, he didn't want to think about Kristin Taylor. She wasn't a part of his life anymore. He'd made that abundantly clear when he realized the extent of his injuries and the length of his recuperation. Kristin had claimed she loved him, that the accident didn't make any difference in their relationship. Maybe she'd thought she meant it, but Cole had known it would be difficult for her to marry a man who couldn't maintain his celebrity status.

He was aware of the fact that she'd become involved with one of his old teammates, even though she kept calling him and showing up unexpectedly from time to time. She insisted she still loved him and wanted to share his future. But Cole was nobody's fool. He realized that the phone calls and visits had started again after two major networks had offered him jobs as a TV sportscaster. If he decided to take one of the offers, he could have Kristin back. As a sportscaster, he could still be a part of the life he'd once enjoyed, as well as earn a top-notch salary. Having Kristin back would mean a dazzling blonde on his arm in public and a talented lover to entertain him in private. He wasn't sure whether or not he wanted the sportscasting job, but he was damn sure he didn't want Kristin.

Well, it wasn't as if he had to decide about the job to-night, or tomorrow or even next week. He had almost two months, until Christmas, to make a decision that would affect his entire future. That's why he was here, a hundred and fifty miles from his hometown of Memphis, seeking solitude at Holly House. Somehow he doubted his stay here would be peaceful. The sultry Widow Darnell stirred his blood, the very sight of her arousing all his male instincts. From the moment he'd seen her in the glow from his cigarette lighter, he'd wondered what it would be like to hold her in his arms, to kiss her long and hard, to take her to his bed and love her thoroughly. Just the thought of that curly, Titian hair spread across an ivory pillow stirred his manhood to life.

What he needed was a bath and a good night's sleep. Tomorrow Lucky would look just like any other pretty woman. If she didn't then he knew he'd have only two choices. Either he'd have to leave, or make love to the mistress of the house.

Cole unbuttoned his shirt quickly and threw it onto a nearby rocking chair. He rubbed his stiff neck, turning it from side to side. He scratched his chest, then lowered his fingers to unbuckle his belt. He heard a gasping sound from the doorway and looked up to see Lucky standing there, her gaze fixed on his chest. His erection stiffened even more.

He'd never seen anything as utterly beautiful as the woman whose curvaceous body beckoned to him. Her bright auburn hair hung in loose curls to her shoulder blades. Her beguiling blue-gray eyes devoured him with longing, running over his hard, muscular torso as if they'd never seen a partially nude male form. Her full, sensuous mouth parted, and her nostrils flared while she took in one labored breath after another. Her chest rose and fell with tantalizing movements, her lush breasts straining against her yellow blouse.

Cole yearned to touch her, run his hands down her womanly hips, clutch her by the buttocks and pull her to him. He could almost feel her soft, sweet body pressing against his throbbing need.

"Lucky?"

She stood in the doorway with two towels, a washcloth, and an unwrapped bar of soap in her hands. She knew she shouldn't be staring at him, inspecting every inch of his broad, hairy chest, but her eyes refused to give up the pleasure. She'd been around men all her life. She'd been married for five years, but never had the sight of a man's naked chest taken her breath away. Her fingers itched to touch him, to glide through the thicket of black hair that covered Cole Kendrick from neck to waist.

"I...I...here's the towels and soap." Lucky laid the items on a mahogany tilt-top table near the door.

"Lucky?"

No, no, her mind screamed. Don't answer that invitation you see in his eyes, that you feel emanating from his big, aroused body. "Good night, Mr. Kendrick."

Lucky turned and ran, leaving Cole staring into the darkness. "Good night, Ms. Darnell. I'll see you in the morning," he said into the empty stillness that surrounded him.

Two

Cole didn't know if it was the sound of Strauss waltzes floating up the stairs or the smell of delicious home-baked bread filling the air that stirred his curiosity the most. After tossing and turning half the night, he'd finally fallen asleep around dawn, only to be awakened before seven by the sound of a lawn mower. As he walked carefully down the back staircase, he hoped that Lucky Darnell's night had been as bad as his. He moved down the hallway, the lilt of violins growing louder and louder with each step. He told himself that everything would be all right. Once he saw the woman whose image had plagued his thoughts during the night, he'd realize there was nothing special about her. She was just another good-looking redhead. One whose silvery eyes could see straight to a man's soul and heat his passions to the boiling point.

Cole turned the glass doorknob, opening the French door. He stood watching Lucky as she bent over and

reached into the oven of the old cookstove that stood on a
raised hearth in the corner of the kitchen. Cole let his gaze
travel slowly over the fullness of her buttocks as they
strained against a pair of paint-stained jeans. Her legs
weren't long, but they were shapely, her ankles trim and
her feet small. Cole wondered just how tall she was. About
five-five, he guessed. Last night when they'd stood in the
lamplight staring at each other, she'd come just about to
his chin, and he was six feet tall.

He watched as she pulled a glass loaf pan from the oven
and set it on top of the stove. A lavender ribbon tied back
her long, curly hair into a loose ponytail.

She closed the oven door with the side of her hip and
turned around. She pulled a small hand towel off her
shoulder, wiped her hands and looked up to see Cole
standing in the doorway, his dark eyes surveying her from
head to toe. Suddenly all the blood seemed to rush from
her head and go directly to her cheeks.

"Good morning, Mr. Kendrick. What would you like
for breakfast?"

He leaned against the doorpost, taking a casual stance
as he crossed one leg over the other. "I'm not much of a
breakfast eater. I don't usually get up this early, but some
kid with a lawn mower wasn't aware of my sleeping hab-
its."

Lucky tried to smile. She threw the towel back across her
shoulder and picked her coffee mug up off the nearby
counter. "I'm sorry Joel woke you, but if you'll remember, you aren't supposed to be here until this afternoon.
I've got a lot of work to do to get the grounds looking
good before the grand opening of Holly House Antiques."

Cole held up a hand as if defending himself. "Hey, I
wasn't blaming anybody. It'll probably be good for me to

get up early while I'm living in the country for the next few weeks.''

"I'd hardly call a mile from the heart of downtown Florence 'the country.' But you're right. Getting up early is good for you. Mornings are the best time to get started.''

Cole pushed away from the doorpost and took a few sauntering steps toward Lucky, his limp barely noticeable. "We've got a slight difference of opinion. I'm definitely an afternoon man myself. But since fate has decreed a change in my life this morning, I could use some caffeine to help me wake up.''

Lucky set her mug down and flipped off the cassette player on the counter. She took another mug from the wooden rack beside the coffee maker and filled it. "If you want breakfast, I need to fix it now because I've got to get outside soon.''

"Just a cup of coffee." Cole eyed the three loaves of golden-crusted bread cooling on the museum-piece stove. He'd never smelled anything that tempted his taste buds the way the aroma of Lucky's bread did.

"Would you like a couple of pieces of my sourdough bread? It's still warm.''

"With butter and jelly?''

"With butter and homemade strawberry preserves.''

When Cole sat down at the kitchen table, he noticed playing cards spread out in a game of solitaire, half the cards still in the deck. "Were you playing?''

"Guilty," Lucky said as she placed the coffee mug in front of him. "Cards are my big sin. Uncle Pudge taught me to play poker when I was four, and I've been addicted ever since.''

Cole laughed, deep, rumbling chuckles that deepened the grooves along the sides of his wide mouth. "Have you just revealed your darkest secret?''

"Let's say that I've given you fair warning.''

Cole continued smiling while Lucky placed two huge slices of bread on a paper towel and laid it on the table. "Should I be making a connection between what you just said and your name?"

Putting a jar of preserves and a dish of butter beside the bread, Lucky sat down to her card game. "About the only way you could beat me at cards would be to cheat the way Uncle Pudge always does."

"Is it true?" he asked.

"Is what true?"

"That old saying about being lucky in cards and unlucky in love?"

Lucky picked up the deck of cards. Her eyes were clear and void of any emotion when she spoke. "I was very lucky once."

"Maybe you will be again."

"Maybe."

Cole picked up one slice of bread and broke it in two. Lucky handed him a sturdy plastic knife. "Sorry about the utensils, but it'll save me cleanup time," she said as she began flipping over the cards.

Cole spread butter and sweet red preserves on the bread. "Most of the women I've known wouldn't have any idea how to bake homemade bread." He took a huge bite, savoring the unique fermented taste.

"It comes from having been raised by my grandmother. I can cook, sew, crochet, knit, can fruits and vegetables—"

"My God, the perfect homemaker." Cole hadn't meant the words to sound so condemning, but realized Lucky had been offended by his tone when she plopped down several cards with a resounding thud.

She placed the red seven on the black eight, then the two of hearts on the ace. She rested her elbows on the table and scowled at Cole Kendrick. "I'm not a perfect anything, but you're right. I am a good homemaker, a damn good homemaker, and I'm sick and tired of people implying that something's wrong if you're a woman under fifty and haven't become the president of a major corporation."

With his mouth half-full, Cole tried to reply. "Sorry, I didn't—"

"That's what's wrong with this country. Half the men want their wives to be nothing but a little housewife, and the other half want a sexual relationship with a woman financially able to support them. What I'd like to see is a man willing to accept a woman for who and what she is, willing to appreciate old-fashioned qualities while encouraging her to fulfill herself creatively."

Cole swallowed several gulps of coffee, then burst into loud, gut-wrenching laughter.

Lucky threw the cards down, raked them into a pile and restored order to the deck. "Just what's so funny?" She slammed the cards down on the table, knotted her hands into fists and glared at Cole with eyes like molten steel.

He reached out and took both her clenched fists into his big hands. She jerked them back, but he grabbed and held on tightly. "Lady, you take offense mighty easy. Or is it that I happen to rub you the wrong way?"

Lucky pulled on her captured fists. Biting down on her tongue, she closed her eyes and silently counted to ten. "You...don't...affect me in any way," she said, her teeth clenched.

"Oh, but I think I do. I think I affect you in every way a man can affect a woman." Cole transferred both of her hands into one of his. "I'd like to rub you in all the right ways."

"I'm not interested in you doing anything to me. I'm not some little baseball groupie out for a one-night stand. I'm not even a fan. I hate baseball and I don't like you."

Ever so gently Cole clasped one of her wrists in his free hand, allowing his thumb to rest on the underside. "Oh, I think you like me, Lucky, and that's what's bothering you. How long's it been since you've had a man?" His thumb began a slow crawl up the inside of her arm.

Lucky swallowed, her lips trembling, parting on a refrained sigh. "Let...go...of...me." She enunciated each word separately, her teeth clenched so tightly her jaws ached. She wanted nothing more than to slap his handsome face.

"Have you been with a man since your husband died?"

"That's none of your business."

"Are you sleeping with the good doctor?"

"Why, you—"

"He must not be much of a lover, or you wouldn't still be so hungry."

"Rich is twice the man you are. He's kind and gentle and considerate. He's a gentleman. Obviously something you know nothing about." Lucky tugged on her hands so hard that she bounced in her seat, the chair popping up off the floor then falling back down.

"You got that right. A boy who grows up on the streets of Memphis learns how to be a man before he's through puberty. Survival is the name of the game, not good manners and small talk."

She stared at him, seeing for one brief second the small, insecure child he once must have been. Somewhere inside Cole was a boy in pain. All her loving and maternal instincts came to focus on the man whose crude words had baited her to fight.

"Sometimes I'm not much of a lady. Granny always told me that a real lady never loses her temper, and most certainly never argues with a gentleman."

"I think we've both already agreed that I'm not a gentleman, so all you've done is defend yourself against a man who was deliberately trying to provoke you."

She let her clenched fists relax within his hold. He squeezed her hands gently. "Why would you want to provoke me?"

Cole's thumb worked its way up under the sleeve of her lavender sweater. He'd never felt anything as soft and warm as this woman's skin. "I want to be honest with you. I...I know it's crazy, but I think I'm as afraid of you as you are of me."

"I'm not afraid—"

He released his tenacious grip on her hands, letting them fall free as he covered her lips with two big fingers, and his other hand grabbed her shoulder, pulling her closer to him. "The one thing we don't need is to lie to each other."

Lucky looked at Cole, the sound of her own heartbeat thundering in her ears. "I've never...the way I feel...I...I don't understand. Why now? Why you?"

For endless moments, they simply looked at each other, neither of them speaking. It was as if they both realized that words would only get in the way, create problems that they weren't able to deal with right now. With his thumb pressed between the inside of her arm and the rounded curve of her breast, Cole fondled her. His other hand glided from her shoulder upward, encircling her slender neck. Boldly they inspected each other.

Lucky placed her palm against his stubble-roughened cheek. His face intrigued her, and, as if her fingers had sight, they learned his features one by one. By the time she reached his ears, her hand was trembling with an excitement that raced through her body, quickly reaching the core of her sensuality.

Cole wanted her, wanted her now, in the kitchen, on the table with bright, autumn sunshine pouring through the windows. He hadn't felt such an animalistic need since he'd been a teenager in a perpetual state of arousal. Would she be shocked, he wondered, if she knew what he was thinking? Somehow he doubted it. Not if he was correctly reading the subtle changes in her body, the look of yearning in her eyes, the touch of hunger in her fingertips.

With not one word spoken, without one touch of true intimacy, Lucky and Cole made love. Within the deepest, most private part of their minds, they joined, and this special joining created a hunger within them for a physical union they had to deny themselves.

The back door leading to the screened porch swung open, and a tall, gangly teenage boy stepped inside the kitchen, sweat staining his white T-shirt and flecks of freshly cut grass dotting his worn jeans. "I've finished the mowing. You ready for us to start raking?"

The sound of Joel Haney's voice destroyed the spell of sensuality captivating Lucky. She pulled away from Cole and clutched her body in a protective hug. Taking several deep, calming breaths, she looked up at the young man who was curiously glancing back and forth from her to Cole.

"Why don't you get a cola and take a rest first." Lucky forced a smile to her lips. "You can meet Holly House's first guest."

Joel followed her instructions and joined them at the table. He appraised the man sitting across from him, his clear blue eyes frankly hostile. "You're that big-time ball player that nearly got killed in a car wreck a couple of years ago, aren't you?"

Lucky knew Joel was being deliberately rude, but couldn't bring herself to chastise him. Obviously he'd seen just enough to ignite the type of jealousy only a sixteen-year-old with a crush could feel. And since Joel considered her one of his few true friends, he felt quite protective of her.

"Cole Kendrick." Cole held out his hand to the boy, man-to-man.

Joel looked at the big outstretched hand, hesitated, looked at Lucky, then exchanged a quick handshake. "I'm Joel Haney. I'm a friend of Lucky's. A good friend."

"Hey, why don't I grab myself a cola, and you and I go on outside and take a look at that flower bed where I want to plant the tulip bulbs?" Lucky needed to escape. The last thing she wanted was to contend with these two male adversaries when she had so much work to do, so much to accomplish in so short a time.

Lucky leaned against the ancient oak tree, pulled off her work gloves and stuck them in her back pocket. Lifting her ponytail, she stretched her neck, turning it from side to side, enjoying the feel of the cooling breeze as it touched her damp skin.

She and Joel had been working for hours, raking dead grass and leaves, trimming shrubbery, weeding the marigolds along the back walk and preparing the flower beds for spring. They had taken special care with all the holly bushes from which Holly House had taken its name. The glorious, green shrubs gave the grounds a perpetual verdancy, even in the dead of winter.

There was still so much to do before she could open Holly House to the public. If her triple-part plan worked, she'd not only be able to keep her grandmother's ancestral home, but she'd also be able to make the repairs and maintain the fourteen-room mansion and the twenty acres that still belonged to her family. But if she didn't succeed? No, she wouldn't allow herself to let any negative thoughts cloud her vision of a bright future.

Joel approached her, a tall glass of iced tea in his grubby hand. "Here. Uncle Pudge sent this out to you. He said him and that Kendrick fellow are about ready for lunch."

"What time is it?" She looked at the inexpensive digital watch on her wrist. "Good grief, it's nearly two-thirty."

"I thought Holly House was going to be a bed and breakfast sort of place." Joel handed her the glass.

"It is, why?"

"Then you're not responsible for fixing that man lunch or supper every day."

"Oh, I see." Lucky bent to her knees, then sat down on the ground, bracing her back against the tree. "Well, Mr. Kendrick is a special guest. He's paying double what I plan to charge next spring. So, when I cook, he'll be joining us."

"Why's he paying so much to stay here when you haven't even got the place ready yet?"

"Look, honey," she said as Joel sat down beside her. "Cole Kendrick's reasons for being here are his private business, don't you think?"

"Well, hell, Lucky. I don't think it's a good idea him being here and all. I don't like the way he looks at you. A guy like that wouldn't have the first idea about how to treat a lady like you." Joel looked at Lucky, the adoration in his eyes so obvious that she wanted to cry.

She took the boy's dirty hand in hers and squeezed, hoping she could reassure her valiant young protector. "Don't worry about me. I'm perfectly capable of taking care of myself. Besides, I want you concentrating on schoolwork. I'm expecting you to make the honor roll by the end of this year."

"The honor roll? You sure do expect a lot out of a guy. Are you forgetting I just learned how to read two years ago?"

Lucky grinned, remembering the surly fourteen-year-old who had resented every effort she'd made to help him. He'd been ashamed to admit he read at a first-grade level when he was a high-school freshman. Living at below poverty level, with a drunken father and no mother, had ill prepared Joel for public education. If he hadn't come to work as a gardener for her grandmother, he'd still be lost in the dismal world of illiteracy.

"I haven't forgotten your ability. What you've achieved in the past two years is nothing short of remarkable."

"Thanks to you and your grandmother. Why somebody like me mattered to that old woman, I'll never know."

"Granny liked you. She told me you were a good boy, but you hadn't had any raising."

"Yeah, she had a way of getting right to the heart of the matter. Nothing's ever going to change my past. A guy like me will never be good enough. Just like that Kendrick. Even if he is rich and famous now, everybody knows that he was just a streetwise kid from the slums of Memphis. The only reason he made it was because he can hit a baseball."

Lucky finished the last drops of tea, letting moisture from the ice cubes drizzle down her chin. "Is that why you've taken a disliking to Cole, because he reminds you of yourself?"

Joel cocked a bushy golden brow, his blue eyes widening in an aren't-you-smart expression. "You know the old saying. It takes one to know one."

"Then you should know that even bruised and ugly apples can make some awfully good cider if the proper care is taken in preparation. And since you've tasted my cider, you know I'm an expert on the subject."

"You better not be getting any notions in your head that all Kendrick needs is the love of a good woman. Even if it was the truth, how do you know he can give you what a woman like you needs?''

Lucky could never quite get used to Joel's manly act. The tough life he'd led seemed to rob him of a real teenage experience. ''I don't fit well on a pedestal, honey.'' Lucky handed him the empty tea glass and stood up. ''I'm thirty years old. I'm not some moonstruck little girl who's going to be seduced by a worldly celebrity. Quit worrying about me.''

''Why is it that sometimes I feel like your father?'' Joel asked, getting to his feet.

''Because you're old before your time.'' So is Cole Kendrick, she thought. If all the publicity releases about Cole's impoverished background were true, then he and Joel did indeed have a great deal in common. Perhaps there was some way the man and the boy could help each other, kindred souls sharing a common pain.

''So what about lunch?''

''Go on in and tell Uncle Pudge I'm almost through out here for now. We can plant the rest of the bulbs later this afternoon. I've got fifty more bulbs I want to plant along the entrance drive.''

''Can I help you finish up?''

''No. I can handle it.''

''Okay,'' Joel said as he started walking away.

Lucky picked up two metal rakes and laid them across the wheelbarrow, then pushed the load of unused mulch toward the old carriage house.

Shards of sunlight shot through rotted, broken boards of the structure, allowing her to see a clear path into the building that had been used as a shed for the past fifty years. The smell of black, rich earth and damp mold blended with the more subtle aroma of aged wood and rusting metal.

Lucky took her time putting things away as she enjoyed the solitude and shadowy stillness. She needed time to prepare herself to see Cole again. Would he look at her with those hot eyes and melt her resistance? The last thing she needed in her life right now was to fall in love. Even if the man who ignited such desire within her was someone with whom she could build a future, this was the wrong time for romance. No one, not even Uncle Pudge, knew how much was riding on the success of Holly House Antiques and the bed and breakfast next spring. There hadn't been any need to worry him about something he couldn't change. He didn't have the kind of money it would take to save Holly House, and if her plans failed, neither would she. The next payment was due in January. If she didn't have it . . . No, she would not let herself think about the alternative.

"Daydreaming?" a husky masculine voice asked.

Lucky jerked, startled by Cole's presence. He stood just inside the doorway, the noonday sun behind him, framing his big body with shimmering light. His eyes held a dark predatory gleam that both frightened and excited her.

"I . . . I told Joel to let Uncle Pudge know I'd get lunch ready as soon as I finished up out here." She pulled the work gloves out of her back pocket and placed them on a small wooden shelf.

"I haven't seen Pudge in over an hour. I've been in my room doing exercises." He moved farther into the building, stopping less than a foot from Lucky.

The thought of all those muscles pushing, straining, pulsating as he exercised made her feel hot and cold all at the same time. The sight of his broad, hairy chest the way she'd seen it last night flashed through her mind. "Oh." The word wasn't much more than a whisper.

Cole turned his head from side to side, giving the interior a brief inspection. "What was this place, the stables?" he asked.

"It was the carriage house, but it's been used as a sort of junk house since my mother was a child. I'd like to convert it into a garage one of these days."

"I wish it was one now. I didn't stop to think you might not have a garage when I drove the Corvette down. I'm afraid she's used to being pampered."

"It's a beautiful car." Lucky's full, pink lips parted as she smiled. "I have to confess that Joel and I took a close look. We decided it's a '59. Right?"

"Right. She's my dream car. I can remember the first time I saw one." Just for a moment, a wistful expression stole across his face, but was quickly gone, a meditative scowl tightening his handsome features. "I promised myself that someday I'd own a car just like it."

"And now you do," Lucky lifted the rakes from the wheelbarrow and hung them on the back wall.

"Yeah. I was blessed with an ability that made me a millionaire in my twenties. Not bad for a guy whose old man lived on disability checks." The filtered sunlight touched his sooty brown hair, lightening the strands to a dusty bronze.

She turned as he took a step forward. Their bodies collided, jolting Lucky so that she grabbed Cole's shoulders for support.

"I...I didn't know you were so close." When his big hands gripped her waist, a shudder passed through her, and she wrenched her eyes away from his, focusing on the spot where his chest met her breasts.

"I'll bet you were a pretty little girl," he said, nuzzling her flushed cheek with the tip of his nose. "I can see you in frilly dresses, playing, laughing, that red hair flying as you ran up and down the steps in that big old house. I guess you were your daddy's darling, weren't you?''

Lucky closed her eyes. His nearness disturbed her in every way possible, and the feel of his day's growth of beard abrasively rubbing against her soft skin was driving her crazy. "My daddy wasn't here. My parents divorced when I was five. My father's daughter by his second wife is his darling."

"I'm sorry," he whispered, his warm breath fanning her ear. "I know what it's like to have only one parent. My kid sister and I grew up without a mother."

"I was more fortunate than most children from broken homes. I had Granny and Uncle Pudge as well as a loving mother. I grew up very happy here at Holly House. This place means everything to me."

"It must be wonderful to have such good memories." His hand moved slowly over her back, stroking, gently caressing.

Lucky fought an overwhelming need to kiss him. Never in her life had she longed to take the initiative, but this man brought out the most basic instincts in her.

"I've lost everyone I've ever loved except Uncle Pudge. My father, Mother, Granny...Greg. I won't ever lose Holly House, no matter what I have to do to keep it."

"I can't imagine caring so much about an old house and a few acres of land." He felt her stiffen and immediately regretted his choice of words. "Maybe I'm jealous."

"Of what?" Her whole being seemed to be filled with an unknown urgency, as if it were waiting for something that had always been just beyond her reach.

"Jealous of you because you have something you care for so fervently, and jealous of Holly House because I wonder how it would feel to have the passion you feel for this place focused on me."

She could hear his heart beating loud and strong, and wished she could stay here in his arms, feeling safe and protected for the first time in years.

"Did you love your husband like that? With all your heart and soul? Do you still love him?" Cole's lips were in her hair, his breath hot and ragged as his lungs took in short, quick gulps of air.

Unable to stop herself, she clutched the firm muscles covering his shoulder blades as longing so intense it was painful shot through her. She ached to know this man, to have him touch her intimately, to come to her and fill her emptiness.

"Greg...Greg was..." She whimpered when Cole kissed her lightly, starting with one cheek, then moving over her lips to the other cheek. "I'll always cherish...his... memory, but I don't...love him...anymore."

Lucky wondered why she wanted to tell this man, this stranger, that, although she'd loved Greg Darnell with all the sweet stirrings of a first romance, he'd never ignited her slumbering passions. Not even when they'd made love had she known such intense longing as she felt in Cole's arms now. Perhaps she should feel ashamed, but she didn't. She couldn't. Nothing had ever felt so right.

"What about Brewster?" Cole's lips seared her throat. The feel of her hot, sweet body aroused him. His maleness throbbed against her stomach.

"We're just good friends." The words came out in a rushed sigh.

"Good." While one hand held her to him, the other gripped her chin. "Open your eyes and look at me."

She obeyed his command, and her gaze locked with his. No man had ever looked at her the way Cole was, as if his life depended on her response. It was almost terrifying to see such raw hunger. Greg had been so gentle, so undemanding. "Is there someone? Someone you love?" she asked, praying for a negative answer.

"No one."

She expected his mouth to possess hers with the kind of brutal force she saw in his eyes, and was totally surprised when his tongue slid across her lips in slow, repetitive moves that made her throb in the secret recesses of her womanly body. When his tongue touched her teeth, her lips parted, inviting him in. He accepted the invitation with several quick thrusts . . . in and out . . . in and out.

Lucky moaned, her own tongue instinctively joining in a mutually satisfying mating dance. Cole deepened the kiss as his hands massaged her hips, moving gradually to encompass her buttocks and bring her femininity against his pulsating arousal.

She pulled her mouth from his, her breathing erratic, her eyes wild with desire. "Oh, God, Cole, this is too much, too fast. I . . . I . . ." Tears misted her eyes. She laid her head on his chest, her lips pressed against his shirt.

"Shh . . . shh. It's all right. Just let me hold you. I need to feel you close to me this way."

While the hard maleness of him throbbed against her, his hands smoothed over the outline of her body from neck to hips. Her small hands clung to his shirtfront. Hesitantly she inserted a finger between the buttons and rubbed the springy black hair on his chest. Then a second and third finger joined in the pleasure, popping the shirt open.

"That's it, honey, touch me. Last night I couldn't sleep for thinking about the way you looked at my chest when you found me with my shirt off."

Lucky unbuttoned several more buttons and spread back the soft cotton material. She ran the palm of her hand over his chest, her fingers playing with the thick swirls of hair. "Last night I wanted to touch you like this. It frightened me because I'd never felt . . . never felt anything like it . . . such strong wanting."

"Desire," he said, and once again his lips met hers. This time the kiss was an uncontrollable fire consuming them both.

One small part of Lucky's brain still functioned, the rest of her lost to the drugging influence of Cole's masculinity. She knew if she didn't stop now, it would be too late. As much as she wanted to know his complete possession, she realized they were little more than strangers. Two people undeniably attracted to each other, but people from different worlds, with totally different goals. She couldn't let anything, not even her feelings for Cole, interfere with saving Holly House.

She pulled free from his magnetic kiss. "Cole, please."

"You're not ready, are you? Emotionally, I mean." He ran his big hands up and down her arms while he sucked in several deep breaths. "It's all right. I should have known a woman like you couldn't act on just a physical level."

"I've never had sex with a man I didn't love. I want you, but I don't know you. I've already lost so much, Cole, been hurt so many times. I—"

"Go on in the house and fix Uncle Pudge's lunch. I'll be in later when my body is back to normal." He tried to laugh, but it sounded more like a grunt. "I can wait. When the time's right, you'll let me know."

"And if the time is never right?" she asked as she turned to go.

"Then we'll both wonder for the rest of our lives, won't we?" Her warm, caring eyes reflected pain.

He stood unmoving for endless moments after she left. His hard male body was primed and ready to perform, but the partner of his choice was gone. Quickly he rebuttoned his shirt, trying not to remember the feel of her soft hands on his flesh.

He'd known quite a few women in his youth and had had several satisfying affairs over the years, culminating in his engagement to Kristin nearly three years ago, but he'd never experienced anything like this. He felt as if he'd been hit in the stomach with a fastball. He wondered if he should have told Lucky about his ex-fiancée, then decided it couldn't possibly matter to her. After all, he assured himself, he wasn't committed to either woman, even if his heart was trying to tell him something different.

Three

Lucky sat alone in her cozy den. She curled up on the chintz sofa and listened to Beethoven's Symphony no. 5 in C Minor. As the music filled the room and encompassed her in its timeless magic, she began to relax.

The past week had been the longest one of her life. Each day started at five and ended when she was too exhausted to work any more. Crews of carpenters and painters littered the downstairs areas of Holly House, giving Uncle Pudge an excuse to fuss and fume. Even though her uncle knew she was doing the only sensible thing, moving her antique business to save the huge monthly rent on a downtown building, he was finding it difficult to adjust to the idea that hordes of people would soon be invading his home.

Lucky fervently hoped that the dreaded mass of customers would indeed appear on a regular basis when she opened Holly House Antiques, and that those patrons would bring friends back for the weekend tours of the house and grounds, which she had planned to bring in extra revenue. And if everything worked out, word of mouth would prove to be a major source of advertisement when she opened the bed and breakfast.

She hadn't found it difficult to avoid her guest during the past six days. She saw him briefly each morning when he joined Uncle Pudge and her for breakfast, but the rest of her day was always so filled with a series of mental struggles and physical labor that she saw Cole only occasionally. Every night she took a long soak in her claw-foot bathtub, then fell into Granny's tester bed and prayed for a few hours sleep before having to face another workday.

Several times she'd caught Cole Kendrick standing at a distance, his dark eyes surveying her from head to toe. His slow, speculative looks unnerved her because she knew he was remembering the kisses they'd shared in the carriage house. She wished she could forget those kisses, forget the way they made her feel. This was the wrong time for romance to enter her life again, and Cole was definitely the wrong man.

Lucky stood up, stretched and looked at the empty fireplace. On a night like this, there should be a bright, warm fire, she thought. Yet it didn't seem worth the effort. Romantic firelight was meant to be shared.

A Tchaikovsky symphony began, and she walked around the room. Restlessness and exhaustion warred within her. As she neared the fireplace, the strikingly beautiful charcoal drawing of Holly House that hung over the brown marble mantel caught her eye. Joel has a rare talent, she thought. He'd given her the drawing for a birthday gift, and she would never forget the look on the boy's face when she'd shown him the matted and framed picture hanging in such a prominent place in her home.

She wanted Joel to be happy and successful, but doubted he had much of a chance as long as he remained with his father. Lucky knew that a lot of successful people came from poverty-stricken backgrounds. Cole Kendrick, for example. Thanks to the tabloids, the whole world knew Cole probably never would have escaped the slums if he hadn't excelled in high-school sports and been offered a baseball scholarship to Stanford University. Now he was a millionaire several times over. But was he the man to set forth as a role model for Joel?

Restlessness finally won out over exhaustion. Lucky went into the kitchen and set the coffee maker. While the coffee brewed, she gazed out the kitchen window into the moonlit darkness. She could hear strains of Symphony no. 6 in B Minor drifting into the kitchen from the den stereo. She felt so alone here in this big old house. Uncle Pudge had taken Cole to his lady friend Miss Winnie's for supper, and she had no idea when either of them would be home.

No matter how hard she tried, she couldn't stop thinking about Cole. Every time she closed her eyes, she could see him standing, naked to the waist, his hairy chest beckoning her fingers to reach out and touch. She'd never been attracted to rowdy, macho types. In fact, she had shied away from the few diamond-in-the-rough males with whom she'd come in contact.

Gregory Darnell had been her perfect mate, a man whose tastes and background paralleled her own. Their life together had been filled with peace and contentment, and their lovemaking had been as sweet and tender as their feelings for each other. The thought of wanting another man so desperately filled her heart with guilt. Her desire for Cole was a betrayal of her love for Greg. Her mind knew the foolishness of her thoughts, but her heart didn't.

Dear Lord, her whole life was topsy-turvy! She was moving her antique shop, betting every dime she had on making Holly House a paying enterprise...and she was entertaining thoughts of making love to a man she barely knew.

Lucky jerked her head up and placed the palms of both hands on her warm cheeks. She must be losing her mind, she decided. Sex was something she'd enjoyed during her marriage, but she wasn't dying of deprivation. Her body had managed to deal with celibacy for quite some time, so why now did she feel an emptiness inside her only a man could fill? And not just any man. She wanted Cole Kendrick.

Cole stood in the dark dining room looking into the kitchen at Lucky. That redheaded witch had plagued his waking hours and haunted his dreams for the past week.

He felt a little like a Peeping Tom as he stood there quietly watching her. She removed her hands from her face, closed her eyes and hugged herself tightly. Her curly hair fell long and free past her shoulders, its Titian brightness shining like polished copper against the pale gray sweater she wore. His eyes traveled the length of her softly rounded body, stopping briefly to enjoy the way her full breasts shaped the clingy knit material

Damn! Every time he looked at this woman, he became aroused. He hadn't been this horny since he was sixteen and would have laid anything female. He wasn't desperate for a woman. He knew dozens who'd give him anything he wanted. All it would take was a simple phone call and the mention of his name. His body ached with wanting, the kind only a woman could ease. But not just any woman. He wanted Lucky Darnell.

He took several steps into the kitchen, cursing the stiffness in his left leg. "Hello," he said, stopping just inside the doorway.

"Oh." She jumped, startled by his sudden appearance. "When did you get home?"

"Just came in the front door."

"I see."

"I enjoyed spending the evening with Pudge and Miss Winnie, but I decided that it was time to discreetly say good-night and leave the lovebirds alone." Cole saw Lucky's mouth curl into a smile, and his own mouth responded in kind. "God, I hope I'm still enjoying life when I'm eighty."

Lucky willed herself not to blush. It was so embarrassing to have this man know what she was thinking. "Uncle Pudge is quite a character, isn't he?" She walked across the kitchen and tried to avoid looking directly at Cole. "I've got some things to clean up in the den. If you'll excuse me—"

"Why don't you let that wait." He moved toward her, his dark eyes willing her acquiescence. "Couldn't we spend some time together? You've been so busy we haven't had a chance to say more than good morning to each other."

"I...I... well..." Tell him no, the sensible part of her mind warned. "Come in the den. I'll clean up and get us some fresh coffee."

He followed her into the small room. Pudge told him it had once been the library, and one full wall of bookshelves attested to the fact. The first thing that caught his eye was the tile-framed fireplace. He wondered why no one had built a fire on such a cool autumn night.

"Please sit down." Lucky picked up the silver tray from the small trunk she used as a table.

"Coffee would be all right, but something...a little stronger would really hit the spot. You know it's pretty chilly out there." Cole surveyed the room, noticing that what he assumed were antiques mixed unobtrusively into the country decor. There was a homey quality about Lucky's den that appealed to him.

"I have some delicious peach brandy." Lucky looked at the barren fireplace.

Cole saw the wistful expression on her face and decided that their thoughts were running in a similar direction. "You get the brandy, and I'll build a fire. Okay?"

When she smiled, her face glowed with a beauty he longed to capture and hold, to cherish for long, endless hours. "Would you change the tape in the stereo, too?"

"Sure." He watched her until she disappeared into the kitchen, then immediately arranged the logs in the fireplace, took several small sticks of kindling and lit them with his cigarette lighter.

Once the fire began to blaze brightly, he walked over to the stereo. All she seemed to have were classical, semi-classical and easy-listening tapes. He liked country and western. Not one Hank Williams, Jr. tape in the bunch, he noted. Well, he wasn't sure what she wanted to hear, and it didn't really matter to him. He chose a tape labeled Mantovani and hoped she'd like it.

Just as the shimmering soft sound of a hundred strings lulled away the quiet, Lucky came in holding two crystal snifters. She looked at the brightly glowing fire, then at Cole. He moved away from the stereo, limping slightly as he walked around the chintz sofa.

She'd never seen a man as devastatingly attractive as Cole was in his tight stone-washed jeans and plaid flannel shirt. His big, powerful body seemed to dominate the room, a room she'd designed as her own private hideaway. She could feel her heart racing wildly in her chest and knew she was making a mistake. She should be running away from this man, not moving toward him, her senses alert with anticipation.

"Please sit down." Lucky nodded toward the sofa.

Cole sat, crossing his legs at the ankles as he leaned back. One big hand reached out and turned off the table lamp, leaving the room bathed in firelight.

Lucky stood in front of him, offering him a snifter. When he accepted, she sat down on the opposite end of the sofa, her gaze wandering from the pinkish gold liquid in her glass to the yellow-orange flames dancing in the fireplace. "Thanks for making the fire. I love it."

Cole swirled the brandy gently, sniffed its fruity aroma and took a small sip. "Mmm...mmm. Not bad. I don't think I've ever drunk peach brandy before."

"It was my grandfather's favorite. These snifters are his. They're part of a set. Granny used them for special occasions."

"Is this a special occasion?" Desire flamed in his eyes as hot and bright as the fire warming the cool night air.

Lucky smiled at him, a soft, utterly feminine smile that turned her eyes to shimmering silver. "It could be. I'd like for us to be friends, Cole. I don't need more than friendship from you or any man at this point in my life. But I realize that I can't keep avoiding you just because I find you attractive."

Cole drew in a deep breath and sat there staring at her, surprise and disbelief evident in his amused expression. "Lady, you don't pull any punches, do you?"

"I speak plainly, a habit from which Mother was never able to break me. I think it's better to get this thing between us out in the open and deal with it. I don't want a one-night stand or a brief affair. I'm just not geared for something like..."

One big finger traced the line of her jaw. "You're a forever-after kind of woman, aren't you?" Without waiting for a reply, he nodded in agreement. "Okay. We'll play this game by your rules, for now."

Lucky rubbed her thumb across her bottom lip as if contemplating some important strategy. "Since we're friends, I want to invite you to a party Halloween night."

"What sort of party?"

"A costume party right here at Holly House."

"Are you forgetting why I came here? If I attend some big social shindig, I'll defeat my purpose of hiding out."

"It's not some social shindig. It's a party for the youth group at church. It's been held here at Holly House since I was a teenager. It's an annual event. Besides, with the proper disguise, no one will know who you are."

Cole eyed her suspiciously, wondering if some ulterior motive lay behind the invitation. "I don't know, I—"

"Why don't we turn your answer into a payoff for a bet?"

"What sort of bet?"

"We'll play five games of draw poker. If I win, you come to the party." Lucky sipped the brandy, cocking her head back to allow the sweet fermented liquid to go down her throat slowly.

"And if I win, what do I get?"

"What do you want?" She laughed, licking the taste of brandy off her lips.

"That, Ms. Darnell, is a loaded question. I'll take a date next weekend. Pudge told me about an antique-car show over in Tuscumbia." He knew it would be ridiculous to refuse to play an innocent card game with this beautiful woman even if Pudge had warned him that she usually won at least seventy-five percent of the time.

Lucky brought out a new deck of playing cards from the end-table drawer. "Here, you open and shuffle. I'll even let you deal."

Cole set his brandy snifter on the trunk and took the cards. "I'm beginning to get suspicious. Does your name really have anything to do with your card-playing abilities?"

Lucky kicked off her slate gray pumps, bent her legs at the knees and put both feet on the sofa. "The bets have been made. Let's play cards."

"Something tells me I've been bamboozled," Cole said as he shuffled the cards. "Thank goodness I didn't bet my lucky cigarette lighter."

"I've wondered about that lighter," she admitted, wiggling around on the sofa trying to get comfortable. "Why does a man who obviously doesn't smoke carry around an expensive lighter?"

Cole dealt their hands, then picked up and studied his cards intently. "I used to smoke," he said, delving into his jeans pocket to retrieve the sterling silver lighter.

Lucky gazed at the shiny object where it lay nestled in his palm. "Was it a gift from someone special?"

"Yeah," he replied, squeezing the lighter tightly before returning it to his pocket. "It was one of the first expensive things I bought for myself."

"If you quit smoking, why do you keep it?"

"It's a reminder." He laid the cards facedown on the trunk. "How many?"

"Three," she said, laying her cards on top of his. "A reminder of why you don't ever want to smoke again?"

"A reminder of how green and ignorant I used to be, a reminder of how far I've come. I don't guess a woman like you could understand that." He knew damn well she had no way of knowing what it was like to have a father addicted to alcohol, who wasted every dime of his disability check on booze.

"Two pair. Kings and eights," she said.

"Beats me."

"There was a time when I wouldn't have understood, but I do now. In the last few years since I met Joel, I've learned a great deal about human beings that you can't learn in books or by staying safely in your own little social circle." Lucky checked the new cards Cole had just dealt her.

"That kid doesn't like me."

"Oh, I don't think that's exactly true." Lucky wanted to comfort the tormented little boy she knew still lived deep within Cole. "Joel thinks you're two of a kind. He's tried to warn me against you."

Neither of them had much of a hand that round, but Cole won with an ace high. He hoped Lucky wasn't aware of his discomfort. He sure as hell didn't want to have to explain to this refined Southern lady why he had so many hang-ups. The tabloids had told so much about his life, true and false, that everybody knew he'd been a slum kid, but he'd never told anyone, not even his ex-fiancée, anything personal about his old man.

"Joel Haney thinks I'm not good enough for you, huh? He could be right." Cole held the deck of playing cards in one hand and reached out to grasp Lucky's chin with the other. "If you're looking for a man with money, I've got that. But if you want a man with a pedigree, I'm—"

"Cole..." She leaned into him as his hand moved to gently encircle her throat.

"And if you're picky about a man's body being perfect..."

Tears sprang into her eyes, and her mouth trembled slightly with a yearning so strong that she couldn't resist lowering her head just enough to brush his hand with her mouth.

"I've got a crippled leg and scars from my hip to my knee." He clenched his teeth and pulled his hand away from her. "I'm probably not your type. You'd better stick with your own kind."

Lucky wanted to scream at him, to tell him that he had no idea what her type of man was because she didn't even know herself. Once, nine years ago, she'd known that Gregory Darnell was the perfect man for her, the Prince Charming she'd been promised. But she was no longer a twenty-one-year-old virgin with stars in her eyes. She was a woman with mature instincts that told her she could never be content with the kind of easy, pleasant relationship she'd had with her husband.

But Lucky didn't say anything, nor did Cole as they played three more hands of draw poker. She won all three games, but hesitated claiming her prize. The silence between them had strained her nerves, making her want to escape his presence, flee from the tension she felt contained in his big body.

"I'll be at your little church party, Ms. Darnell." His voice dripped with icy scorn.

"Forget it," she snapped. "You'd probably be miserable. I was wrong to think a man like you would enjoy something so quaint and wholesome."

He glared at her, his stern brown eyes boring into her with rage. "You have no idea what a man like me would enjoy, but you'd like to find out, wouldn't you?"

Lucky gasped, surprised by the audacity of his question. "I think it's time we said good-night." She jumped to her feet, turning her back to him.

Cole grasped her wrist, hauling her into his lap. She fell on him, her hip pressed against his groin and one breast crushed against his hard chest. She pushed at him, trying to free herself, but he pulled her closer, trapping one of her arms between their bodies as her head fell against his broad shoulder. When her free hand slapped blindly at his chest, he clamped one big hand around her forearm while the other burrowed through her thick hair to secure her neck.

They stared at each other, earthy brown eyes and molten gunmetal ones, like two warriors determined to die before surrendering. They were so close she could feel his hot breath against her face, could smell the manly heat of his body. She squirmed once, twice, like a female animal trapped by her larger and more powerful mate.

"I could force you, and there wouldn't be a damn thing you could do about it." He watched her pale face turn ashen and her body tremble with fear. He didn't want her afraid; he wanted her aroused and ready. "God, don't think I'd actually do something like that. I only want a willing woman."

"I . . . I'm not willing." She squirmed against him, her buttocks rubbing the jutting hardness between his thighs.

"I could make you willing."

"No, I . . ."

"Tell me that you don't want me." The words were a dare.

"I don't . . . I . . ." Tell him you don't want him, her mind screamed. Protect yourself before it's too late. But she couldn't make herself say the four little words that would set her free. No matter how dangerous the truth was, she couldn't deny it.

"We don't have to make love . . . completely . . . if you're not ready. But, God, honey, I need . . . I need just a little bit of you to keep me from going crazy."

His words were more intoxicating than the brandy could ever be, she thought. If only she could trust him not to let things go too far. Better yet, if only she could trust herself to know when to call a halt. "Oh, Cole, I've never . . ."

"You were married. Surely you wanted your husband." His long fingers raked through her hair, drawing her face against his. He rubbed his cheek against hers, then buried his head in her neck, his mouth opening, his tongue bathing her skin with warm moisture.

"It wasn't like this with Greg. I never felt so... I never ached like this."

"You shouldn't say things like that to a man who wants nothing more in life than to bury himself deep inside you."

Lucky moaned as his tongue made its way up her throat and across her jaw to outline her lips in slow, tormenting strokes. "Please... please kiss me."

Needing no other prompting, his lips took hers with a tortured passion born of a desire too long denied. She opened her mouth, allowing his invasion, welcoming his possession. Starvation claimed them. They consumed, stroking, thrusting, taking their fill. Her breathing became ragged. Her swollen breasts heaved against his chest, and her nipples tightened in a painful need to be suckled.

He released her mouth and looked down at her, seeing a woman who was wanting. One big hand covered her breast. She groaned and arched her back, her whole body quivering with reaction. His palm encompassed her breast, squeezing gently. "You feel so good, honey, so good."

"Cole, please..."

"Will you let me look at you? Will you let me see your beautiful breasts?" He eased her sweater upward, revealing her white lace bra.

Lucky stilled his hands. "Let me." She quickly pulled her sweater over her head and tossed it onto the trunk. She loved the look of yearning she saw in his eyes, and knew he wanted to be the one to remove her bra.

He unsnapped the fragile front clasp and very slowly peeled away the wisp of frothy lace. Her full, round breasts fell into his hands like ripe melons. He lowered his head and nuzzled the cleft between the thrusting mounds. "Oh, Lucky, you're so beautiful, so very beautiful."

She reached up and released several buttons on his shirt, her fingers scratching at his hairy chest. "You're beautiful, too, Cole, and I want to see you again."

His shirt immediately joined her sweater. He pulled her to him, rubbing himself against her, his hirsute chest the perfect mate for her smooth flesh. "I want to touch you." He lowered her down on the sofa, hovering above her, his eyes devouring her as his fingers took both nipples, pinching, releasing, pinching again.

Little gasping, choking sounds came from deep in Lucky's throat as she clutched his shoulders, reveling in the hot, wild sensations shooting through her body. She wanted his mouth on her, would die if he didn't taste her soon.

"Looking and touching isn't enough. I want to...I have to taste you, honey." His mouth went to her breast, totally encompassing one nipple as he began to suck.

Pleasure burst within her as he continued to suckle on one breast while his finger flicked back and forth on the other tip. Heat so intense she thought she'd die gathered between her thighs, and she throbbed with a need more overwhelming than anything she'd ever known. She wanted this man to make love to her, to bury himself hard and deep within her. She felt totally empty for the first time in her life and knew that only Cole Kendrick could fill that emptiness.

The sound of her heavy breathing acted like an addictive drug to his senses. "You're soft and silky," he whispered against her breast, "like warm, sweet cream."

She ran her hands over his chest, teasing his nipples, caressing the thick whorls of black hair. "And you're hard and soft at the same time."

"Oh, my beautiful little redhead, I want you."

Her hands reached up into his thick dark hair and pulled his head down to her mouth. "I want you, too, but I'm afraid."

"I'd never hurt you. Not ever." He kissed her with total gentleness. Gradually the kiss intensified, and his tongue went into play, plunging into her while he ground his turgid manhood against the apex of her thighs.

"Oh, I want you," she cried. "I want you, want you!"

Cole groaned as he held her, his big body shaking while he tried to control the hunger destroying him. He knew he could take her now, and it would be the best thing that either of them had ever experienced. But how would she feel in the morning, about him and about herself? He'd promised that he would take only a bit of her, just enough to keep from going crazy, but a little of her wasn't enough ... probably would never be enough.

"Are you ready to have a brief affair?" he whispered, feeling the instant tension in her body. His purely masculine need cursed him for knowing just the right thing to say to dampen her fiery passion.

She pulled slightly away from him. The glow from the firelight coated his body with a bronze sheen. He looked so big, so totally male, it was all she could do to deny herself the pleasure she craved. "No. I ... no."

"We're not going to stop wanting each other."

"I know." Suddenly she felt very naked, very vulnerable. She reached for her sweater.

"Next time I won't stop. I'm not a gentleman. Remember that." He watched as she pulled on the gray sweater and stood up, hesitating for the slightest instant before picking up her bra and shoes from the floor.

"There won't be a next time. I can't let this happen again."

"Oh, yes, there'll be a next time." Even now he could still see the yearning in her eyes. "And neither of us will be able to stop it."

Lucky turned away and walked out of the den. She knew he was right. Sooner or later this thing between them would explode. She only hoped that they'd both be able to pick up the pieces.

Four

————

Lucky poured ginger ale into the enormous glass punch bowl on the end of the parquet-top seventeenth-century table. She smiled as she looked around, pleased with the autumnal ambiance she had created in the normally elegant dining room. The high-back upholstered chairs lined the paneled walls, each draped in orange or black sheeting, with a stuffed spider, cat, pumpkin or witch resting in the seat. A huge candle-lit jack-o'-lantern grinned devilishly from the center of the table, and a dozen tiny paper spiders hung from the crystal chandelier.

Music, though Lucky wondered if anyone in their right mind called that horrendous noise music, blared from a tape deck located in the foyer. She was pleased that so many teenagers had already arrived for the annual youth-group Halloween party. She had counted over twenty-five, and it was only seven-thirty. She hoped that Joel would accept her invitation and attend this year. She knew that

Uncle Pudge was making an effort to become better acquainted with the boy because he felt Joel needed a good masculine influence, something he definitely didn't get from his father.

Just as Lucky turned to go toward the kitchen, a pretty blue-eyed Indian maiden grabbed the empty ginger ale bottle.

"Why don't you let me finish making the punch?" Suzy said, her long black braids bouncing against her shoulders as she danced in place, keeping time to the music's wild beat. "You need to relight the jack-o'-lanterns on the porch. Jimmy Watkins blew them out."

"That boy's full of mischief," Lucky said as she walked into the kitchen.

"He's a jerk," Suzy said.

Lucky rummaged through a kitchen drawer, pulled out a book of matches and tossed them to Suzy. "You go out and light the jack-o'-lanterns while I see what Jimmy's doing now."

Suzy caught the matches and, with a smile and affirmative nod, went out the back door.

Just as Lucky walked into the foyer, a Confederate-uniformed Pudge Prater met her. A tall, slender, green-haired Medusa stood at his side.

"Where in the world is that handsome Cole?" Winnie Robertson asked, dozens of shiny plastic worms dangling in her spray-painted hair, the exact shade of chartreuse as her long slinky dress.

"I don't know," Lucky mumbled. She didn't want to think about Cole. In the past few days since they'd almost made love in the den, she'd deliberately tried to avoid him.

"She's done everything but ask him to leave," Pudge said, slipping Miss Winnie's arm through his. "I think my gal has finally found herself a real man, and she doesn't know what to do with him."

Lucky gasped. She knew her face was turning pink, and she wished there was some way to get her great-uncle to shut up. "Will you hush? What if someone hears you?"

"Any woman in her right mind would take advantage of propinquity. You two are single, mature adults living under the same roof." Winnie's brown eyes sparkled with mischief as she batted her false eyelashes, their long tips brushing against her frosted-green brows.

"Miss Winnie, you're scandalous. I'm not the least bit interested in Mr. Kendrick," Lucky lied, praying that she could escape this meddlesome pair.

"Merciful heavens, Pudge, check this girl's pulse and see if she's still alive," Winnie said in mock horror.

"Will you two go play chaperones and leave me alone? Just because y'all are carrying on an illicit affair doesn't mean everyone should be." Lucky laughed and turned toward the kitchen, not daring to face her great-uncle and his lady friend after making such a comment.

"See here, gal, that was uncalled-for. I've got a good mind to—"

"She was joking, honey pie," Winnie said. "Besides, she's bound to change her mind once she and Cole are having a little illicit affair themselves."

Lucky escaped into the kitchen, where she promptly gathered up a tray filled with sandwiches and took it to the dining room. For the next fifteen minutes, she busied herself preparing the antique table for a bountiful teenage feast.

The harder she tried not to think about Cole, the more she did just that. He and Pudge had spent so much time together, they'd become bosom buddies, and she knew if her great-uncle had his way, he'd see the two of them married before Christmas. The sudden thought of being Cole Kendrick's wife disturbed Lucky because it filled her with a warmth and longing she couldn't allow herself to feel.

By the end of the week, she planned to have all the stock from her downtown shop moved into Holly House, and by the day after Thanksgiving, she would have a grand opening the likes of which Florence, Alabama, had never seen. No one, not even a man whose presence kept her nerves frazzled, was going to prevent her from achieving her goals.

She didn't want to consider the only two alternatives if the holiday season didn't bring in enough money to make the January mortgage payment. She would either have to sell Holly House or borrow plane fare from Miss Winnie to go to Atlantic City. The threat of losing Holly House was the only thing that would ever prompt Lucky to use her card-playing talents at a gambling casino.

Lucky walked into her den and slumped into the Edwardian-style wing chair. She put her elbows on her knees and bent over, placing her face in one uplifted hand. She reached down with the other hand and stroked the satiny softness of the rows of yellow, red and blue ruffles surrounding her gypsy skirt.

This was the first time ever that she dreaded the Halloween party. Absently she removed the deck of tarot cards from her skirt pocket. She wasn't sure what had possessed her to dress up like a gypsy, but once the decision had been made, she decided to amuse the kids by telling fortunes with the cards. She supposed now was as good a time as any to practice some more. She definitely needed a few minutes alone. Cole was sure to show up soon, and then the evening would become an endless game of cat and mouse. If only Rich hadn't had a hospital emergency, she could have used his presence as a shield. Unfortunately she was on her own, and she wasn't a hundred percent sure she could resist Cole again tonight.

Finally having built up her courage, Lucky ventured out of the den and through the crowd milling around in the foyer, dining room and front parlor. Just as she was wondering why she'd ever made the bet with Cole to attend this party, she looked across the room, as if drawn by a will beyond her control, to where a tall, rugged bandit stood in boots, jeans and Western shirt. He had a bandanna tied around the lower half of his face and a Stetson cocked back on his head. He leaned against the wall, his dark eyes fixed on her surprised face.

Why does he have to look so good? she wondered. Those jeans are indecently tight. She jerked her gaze away from his lower body, then felt like crawling under the nearest rock when she realized he was aware of exactly where she'd been looking.

She decided she might as well get it over with, go over and say hello, glad you came and hope you enjoy yourself. But once she stood in front of Cole, she didn't say a word, nor did he.

Cole stared at Lucky, whose costume and mass of flame red curls gave her a look of wild abandon. Huge gold earrings dangled from her ears, and numerous metal bracelets clattered at both her wrists. A yellow cummerbund encircled her tiny waist, and the elastic top of her lacy blouse hung low on her shoulders and revealed a seductive amount of cleavage in front. Cole's fingers itched to jerk the neckline of the blouse upward, or pull the bright blue shawl up and around her throat, and away from its low-slung position about her hips. Even though he realized that he and Pudge were the only two adult males on the premises, he didn't like the idea that so much of Lucky was uncovered and on display.

"Well, it's about time you made an appearance, boy." Pudge and Winnie walked up beside the couple who were silently devouring each other with their eyes.

"I feel like a fool with this bandanna tied around my face, but I figured it was one sure way to keep my identity a secret." Cole moved away from the wall, his big body brushing Lucky's arm when he reached out and touched Winnie's hair. "Miss Winnie, do you have fishing worms in your hair?"

Winnie giggled like a schoolgirl and batted her false eyelashes. "I'll have you know I'm Medusa, and these are green snakes coming out of my head."

"Well, you must have lost your powers because I haven't seen one person who looked like they were made of stone," Cole said as he very casually put his arm around Lucky's waist and drew her close.

Lucky wanted to pull away from him, but she couldn't. She loved the feel of his warm, hard body against her.

"Why don't you two young folks go for a walk outside?" Winnie said, cuddling up to her escort. "Pudge and I have already been for a stroll. The wind's barely cool, and that moon is as big and bright as a sunflower. We even sat in the swing for a while."

"That sounds like a great idea." Cole tightened his hold on Lucky.

"Well, I'll be damned, look who's here," Pudge said, and three sets of eyes followed the old man's gaze toward the front door. Joel Haney, dressed like a scruffy hobo, stepped inside.

"Oh, this is wonderful." Lucky called out the boy's name and waved at him. He saw Lucky, smiled, and within seconds, joined the party.

"I'm so glad you came." Lucky took Joel's hand. "I want you to mix and mingle and have a good time."

The boy's nervous blue eyes darted about the room, then came to rest on Lucky's smiling face. "I don't fit in here. I came because I knew how important it was to you."

"Well, whatever your reason for coming, we're glad you're here," Winnie said, then turned to Pudge. "Come on, honey pie, let's go dance while there's some slow music playing."

"Joel, why don't we go bob for apples," Lucky said, relieved to be escaping from Cole.

"Wasn't exactly what I had in mind, Lucky." Joel glanced over toward Cole, and the man nodded in greeting.

"All right, we'll just walk around, and I'll introduce you to some of these pretty girls," Lucky said, noticing the unspoken exchange between the big man and his young counterpart. It was unnerving the way they seemed able to read each other's minds. If only they liked each other, Lucky thought. She was certain Cole could help Joel on a level she could never reach, a level of common background and similar experiences.

Joel followed Lucky through the house. She stopped to introduce him to every girl there. When they'd made the rounds, Joel leaned back against the wall in the corner of the dining room.

"I feel like an idiot," he said. "Everybody's looking at me like I'm scum. They know I'm nothing like them."

"I don't care if you're not like them. I know you're going to become a man who can be proud of himself."

"Like your lover-boy, Kendrick?"

"Not you, too," Lucky groaned.

"Not me, too, what?"

"Everyone seems to think there's something going on between Cole and me no matter how many times I say there isn't."

"Who's everybody?"

"Uncle Pudge...Winnie...Suzy and now you." Lucky felt a strange tingling at the nape of her neck. She looked across the room and saw Cole standing near the window, his searing brown eyes riveted to her.

"You just named the four people on earth who care the most about you. We know you too well for you to pretend with us. We don't listen to what you say. We watch what you do. And right now you can't take your eyes off our mystery guest."

Lucky closed her eyes and took a deep breath. Gnawing on her bottom lip, she tried to pretend what Joel had said wasn't true. But it was, and they both knew it. There was something about Cole Kendrick that mesmerized her. "And you were worried about making a fool of yourself. I'm the one doing that by gaping at Cole like some love-sick idiot."

"If you're a fool or an idiot, so is Kendrick. He's still staring at you with those hungry eyes. I may be only sixteen, but I've been around. I know when a man's got it bad. If you don't want to give him what he wants, you'd better send him packing soon."

"Joel Haney, you know far too much for a boy your age. And it's a perfect disgrace for me to allow this conversation to continue."

"Ah, bull," Joel said, took Lucky by the arm and maneuvered her through the crowd of teens until they stood directly in front of Cole.

"Lucky needs some fresh air," Joel told the bandit. "I'm going to get some punch and see if anybody will dance with me."

Lucky didn't have time to react before Joel left and Cole took her arm and led her toward the front door.

A cool, early-night breeze caressed Lucky as she stepped out onto the veranda, and her heated flesh welcomed the refreshing touch. Cole led her to the east-side veranda, where they sat down in an enormous wicker settee plumped high with red gingham cushions. Cole placed his arm across the back of the settee. Lucky sat up straight, stiffening her spine, preparing her body for attack. But Cole made no attempt to touch her. Even though she was grateful, she felt a certain sense of disappointment.

"I'm sorry I was so insistent about your attending the party tonight. I know you must be miserable." If she could admit the truth to him, she would have added that she, too, was miserable. Her life had been planned and orderly before Cole arrived. Now she couldn't seem to keep her mind on the tasks at hand for thinking about his compelling, bewitching eyes, his almost-smirky little grin, his big, strong hands and his broad hairy chest.

Cole tugged on the bandanna until it fell around his neck, the point resting in the V of his half-open shirt. "You've been avoiding me for the last few days." And still he didn't try to touch her.

"I've been busy moving the entire contents of an antique shop." She scooted up to the edge of the settee. She wanted to get up and run away, run as fast and as far from Cole as she could go.

"I've missed you." His long arm rested, unmoving, across the back of the settee, and he propped his other hand, open palmed, on the armrest.

"I don't see when you would have had time. Uncle Pudge has been keeping you entertained, even to the point of sharing Miss Winnie's company with you." Lucky clasped her hands together, holding them in her lap, idly stroking her knuckles with her thumb.

"Do you want me to leave?"

"What?"

"I don't want to complicate your life. I don't want to hurt you. If you want me to, I'll pack my things and leave in the morning." His big body tensed, but he made no move to touch Lucky.

She knew she should tell him to go. If he left, she could concentrate totally on saving Holly House. Her mouth opened, and the words formed in her mind. "No," she said as she jumped up and stood rigidly with her back to him. "No, I don't want you to go. Heaven help me, I want you to..." She buried her face in her hands, choking back tears of frustration and fear and need.

Cole reached out and took her hand, pulling her backward. She felt herself about to topple and tried to brace herself by clutching at the settee, but she grabbed a handful of Cole's shirt just as she lost her balance and tumbled backward into his lap. He caught her about the waist, pulling her into his arms while she squirmed to free herself.

"Cole, please let me go."

He nuzzled her neck, moving his lips slowly up the side of her face. He whispered in her ear. "If I stay, we're going to become lovers, and we both know it."

Lucky closed her eyes, took in a deep breath, then released it on a long sigh. "Yes, I know, but . . . but, I won't let you rush me. I'm afraid. We have absolutely nothing to offer each other—our lives are heading in opposite directions."

"Lady, I'm not used to waiting around for a woman. I don't know a damn thing about courting, and I have no intention of starting now."

"I'm sorry if your pride is hurt by my reluctance to hop into bed with you, but I'm more concerned with my self-esteem at the moment." She tried to pull free, but he held her tightly.

"My pride doesn't have a thing to do with it. I hurt with wanting you. I lie awake at night and imagine what it would be like to strip you naked and run my hands over every inch of your body. I can almost taste the sweetness of your skin when I think about kissing you, loving you with my mouth and tongue."

Lucky thought she would faint. His words were weaving a sensually hypnotic spell around her, and her body softened into the hardness of his. She knew what it was like to lie awake and have erotic dreams.

"I can't handle this right now." Lucky tried once again to pull away, and this time Cole released his hold on her. When she stood up, he stood up beside her, but didn't touch her.

"When can you handle it?" he asked, but there was no anger in his voice, only pain.

"I'm not sure. But when it's right, I'll know." She took several tentative steps away from him.

"I'm not a patient man, honey, but I want you in a way I've never wanted anything in my life, so I'll wait."

Lucky walked around to the front veranda and leaned back against a tall, white pillar, her tear-filled eyes gazing out across the yard. While crazy thoughts of running back to Cole and agreeing to share his bed tonight went through her mind, echoes of the past, of her loving husband, her gentle grandmother, her highly moral mother, dampened her wild desires.

Cole stood and watched her walk back into the house. *Hell, if I had any sense at all,* he thought, *I'd pack my bags and go back to Memphis tonight.* What he needed was a couple of nights in the sack with a willing woman—any woman. He didn't have to wait around here for Lucky Darnell to come to terms with her old-fashioned morals. They wanted each other. It was plain and simple. There was no reason for her to complicate matters. They could have a brief, satisfying affair and walk away unharmed. She was right—their lives were heading in opposite directions, but there wasn't any reason they shouldn't enjoy each other while they had the chance.

* * *

"Hey, man, don't shove me," Joel Haney said, moving away from a tall, dark-haired boy. "She wanted to dance with me."

"I told you to stay away from her, you low-life scum. My girl's too good for you to kiss her feet," Jimmy said.

Lucky moved into the dining room as quickly as she could. Just as Joel reached out and grabbed the other teenager by the front of his shirt, Lucky put her hand on his shoulder. He looked at her and released his foe.

"What's going on here?" Lucky asked.

Neither boy spoke. They glared at each other, macho snarls on their lips.

"It's my fault, Lucky," a perky little blond girl said. "I agreed to dance with Joel because I felt sorry for him, and Jimmy got mad."

Lucky knew the girl meant well, but she'd said the worst possible thing. Her thoughtless words would be a death-blow to Joel's fragile male ego.

Joel pulled away from Lucky and ran into the kitchen. She rushed after him, through the kitchen and into the backyard. He was halfway down the front walk, and Cole Kendrick was by his side. Lucky stopped in the shadows near several huge oak trees and listened to two loud voices, one angry and one calm.

"What's it to you, man?" Joel asked.

"Something must have happened for you to come flying around the house and nearly knock me down." Cole remembered what it had been like to be a kid who didn't fit in with polite society.

"I should never have come. I wouldn't have if it hadn't meant so much to Lucky."

"She's a pretty special lady, isn't she?"

"Yeah, and she's too good for you." Joel backed away from Cole as if he expected the man to hit him.

"You're probably right about that. But sometimes a man wants something better than he is, something special."

Joel eyed the big man whose stern face showed no emotion. "Ah, nothing happened inside. Just some jerk accused me of flirting with his girlfriend."

So, Cole thought, Joel Haney and I have more in common than I realized. We're a couple of roughnecks. "You can't let some jerk get to you. You can't let other people decide what kind of man you are. You're as good as he is."

Joel laughed, a sarcastic, you-don't-know-what-you're-talking-about laugh. "My old man is a drunk. We live in a house that's ready to be condemned, and my old lady slept with every guy in Florence before she ran off."

"Pudge told me you were an artist. I've seen your drawing of Holly House. Forget who your parents are. Forget the filth you've lived in. Think about that talent. Use it to get out. I did."

"So what they wrote about you was true, huh? You actually came from the streets?"

"My father got shot up in Korea, but it messed his mind up, too. When my mother died and left him with two kids to raise on a disability check, he started drinking." The two strong males, boy and man, stared at each other, sizing each other up like prizefighters.

"Lucky's not like your other women," Joel said.

"I know she's a lady," Cole said. It surprised him to realize exactly how much he cared about Lucky Darnell. He never wanted to hurt her. It frightened him to think about caring that much for a woman, a woman so different from any other he'd ever known. A woman who would make him wait. Wait until what? Then he remembered her words, *I've never had sex with a man I didn't love.*

"Tell Lucky I'm all right, will ya? I'm going home."

"You think about what I've said. You'll see I'm right."

Joel stopped when he reached the driveway. "Hey, don't hurt her, you hear me?"

Cole didn't answer. He stood and watched a reflection of the boy he'd been twenty years ago. All the old memories flooded his mind. All the bitterness and hatred engulfed him.

When he felt a soft hand on his shoulder, he shook, startled by the touch. He turned to find Lucky, tears flowing down her cheeks, reaching out for him.

"Oh, God, honey." He pulled her into his arms and held her, wanting to hold her there forever, to keep her safe and protect her from every hurt.

"Thank you for...for being so good to Joel." Lucky felt enveloped within the power of Cole's big body. She wasn't afraid of him anymore, or of her feelings for him.

"We better get you back inside. You're supposed to be chaperoning a party."

"Cole?"

He ran his hands over her back, loving the feel of her satiny skin. "When the time's right, we'll know, honey. I want to wait until you're as sure as I am. If we make love, there's going to be more to it than a one-night stand."

"Oh, Cole. Yes." She looked up at him, her warm gray eyes beseeching, pleading for a kiss.

"Damn, woman, I can't kiss you!"

"I...I didn't ask...you to," Lucky said, pulling away from him, hurt by his insensitive words and angry tone.

"If I kiss you, I'll pick you up and carry you inside, past all your guests and straight to my bedroom. Do you understand?"

Lucky smiled. She laughed. She felt wonderful. "Then you'd better wait and kiss me tomorrow after we go to the antique-car show."

With that said, she pulled completely out of his embrace, turned and walked toward the veranda, not once looking back.

Cole smiled. *Well, I'll be damned,* he thought. *I guess I'm going to learn how to court a Southern belle.*

Five

___

"**O**h, Cole, this one's beautiful," Lucky said as they neared the shiny black antique car. "What is it? Look at those red wheels. Surely that's not the original color."

"Mmm...mmm, this is a beauty," Cole said, running his hand along the deep-crown front fender. "This is a '32 Chevy. A deluxe model, I'd say."

"How can you tell it's a deluxe model?" she asked, knowing Cole would explain thoroughly as he had done for the past hour while they'd made their way around Spring Park inspecting the wide variety of antique cars.

"Well, for one thing, look at the side-mounted spare tire. And the hood doors and the cowl lamps are chromium plated."

"Oh, I see." Lucky followed Cole around to the front of the car, becoming more and more impressed with his knowledge of classic cars. The man was a virtual walking encyclopedia on the subject.

Cole ran his fingers over the sleek silver bird adorning the hood. "See this?"

Lucky moved closer. Cole took her hand, linking his fingers through hers. "It's a bird of some kind, isn't it?" she asked.

"Yep. It's an eagle mascot on top of the radiator cap."

"Cole, how and when did you learn so much about old cars?"

"Old cars!" He arched one dark eyebrow in mock disgust. "I'll have you know all these cars are classics, madam. How would you like for me to refer to your antiques as old furniture?"

Lucky laughed, realizing that she would indeed be offended if he ever dared refer to her cherished antiques as old furniture. "Forgive me. I stand corrected."

"I suppose I learned about classic cars for the same reason you learned about antiques. Because I've always been interested in them. There's just something that draws me to them. Once I started making some real money. I started collecting."

She opened the door of the Chevy and looked inside. "Is that a heater?" she asked, eyeing a rather odd-shaped contraption.

"That is a genuine Chevrolet hot-water heater installed for winter-driving comfort."

Lucky ran a hand over the plush driver's seat. "I didn't know you had a collection of classic cars. What do you have besides the '59 Vette?"

Cole put his arm around Lucky's waist, pulled her out of the car and walked with her to the trunk. "I don't have an extensive collection. Right now I only have ten vehicles. I wish you could see them sometime, especially the 1950 Grand Daimler."

"Why especially that one?" she asked, peeping inside the open trunk.

"Because it happens to be the world's largest convertible." Cole couldn't resist leaning his head down to nuzzle the side of Lucky's neck. Her wild, red hair hung in a curly ponytail, exposing her neck and ears. "That's a telescoping trunk you're looking at."

"A what?" Lucky had always considered herself an intelligent woman, but she felt totally ignorant today.

"The back half of the trunk slides rearward to make more room for storage."

"How about that." A shiver passed through her when Cole's lips barely grazed her earlobe. "Cole. Will you stop that. There are people staring at us."

"So. The guys are jealous because they can't nibble on your neck and ears," he whispered, his breath warm and enticing.

"I'd think you wouldn't want to draw attention to yourself. What if someone recognizes you?"

"Hey, I've got on my sunglasses. I'm incognito." He adjusted the stylish aviator sunglasses that he hoped were successfully masking his identity. "Besides, who'd be looking for me at a car show in Tuscumbia, Alabama?"

"Where would people expect to see you?" She didn't like to think about how different their life-styles were, how completely unsuited they were for each other.

"Hitting the hot night spots in some big city with a tall, bosomy blonde on each arm."

Lucky jerked free, swatting him playfully from head to chest. "You poor thing, doomed to spend the afternoon in Spring Park with a short redhead."

Cole grinned, his gaze traveling from her large gray eyes, down her slender neck to the rounded swell of her breasts. The bulk of her sequin-decorated sweatshirt adequately camouflaged her ample endowment. But he well remembered the size and shape and taste of her. "My tastes have changed. I prefer short, bosomy redheads now."

He reached out and pulled her back into his arms, smiling down at her, daring her to withdraw from his embrace.

She put her arm around his waist, tossed her head back and laughed. "Your tastes have improved." Lucky caressed him with her eyes, drinking in the sight of Cole Kendrick. From his Roll Tide red-and-white sweatshirt to his hip-hugging jeans, he was the most masculine creature she'd ever known. "Hey, I'm dying of thirst. Let's go get some coffee or Coke or something."

Arm in arm they walked past several cars, ranging from a 1936 Cord to a golden yellow 1955 T-Bird. When Cole spotted a 1953, two-door Chevy Bel-Air, their direct route to the concession stand was interrupted for ten minutes.

Cole handed Lucky a foam cup filled with steaming black coffee, then reached out to pick up his own.

Lucky took a sip. "Well, at least it's hot."

Crossing the narrow road between the concession stand and the main park area, Cole took a large gulp from his cup. "Woo...ooo! It sure doesn't taste like yours, honey."

They walked past a line of antique trucks as they made their way toward the spring. Ducks swam across the smooth surface of the small lake, and several waddled along the banks, gulping down bread crumbs thrown by two small children and their mother.

"We should have brought something for the ducks," Cole said as they watched the woman and children.

"If I hadn't been so busy this morning, I'd have remembered to bring a loaf of bread."

"If you don't slow down on work, you're going to be in a rest home by the time Holly House Antiques opens."

"Joel and I moved the last few boxes from downtown this morning. He's cleaning up things there this afternoon. My lease on the building officially ended today." Lucky led Cole along a narrow pathway toward a quiet, secluded area at the edge of the lake.

"How's he doing today?" Cole pulled a handkerchief from his back pocket and wiped off the concrete bench before Lucky sat down.

"Oh, Lordy, Cole. I want to help him so much, but he has no self-confidence. It doesn't help, living in a small town where everybody knows who and what his family is."

Cole sat down beside her and put his arm across her shoulders. "It wouldn't matter where he lived, honey. Growing up in Memphis didn't make it any easier having a drunk for a father, no mother and no money."

Lucky heard the pain in his voice, and she knew that, even after all these years, there was a part of Cole still suffering from the ravages of a poverty-stricken childhood.

She longed to comfort him, but wasn't sure he wanted or needed her comfort. Most men had very fragile egos, and the last thing they wanted was a woman to be aware of their weaknesses. If only she knew Cole better, she'd be able to judge his reactions. "While you're here the next few weeks, it would be good for Joel if you'd spend some time with him."

"Are you saying you think he's changed his mind about me?"

"Oh, I think he's always liked you, but he was afraid for me. He sees you and himself as two of a kind. He doesn't think he's good enough for a nice girl, so you're automatically not good enough for me." Lucky finished her coffee and tossed the cup directly into a nearby trash container. "Good shot, huh?"

"A natural athlete." Cole grinned, then finished his coffee and repeated Lucky's toss.

"Can I be nosy?" She laid her head back against his arm, looking up at the clear blue sky.

"About what?" He traced her jawbone, took her chin in one big hand and turned her face toward him.

"You got a phone call right before we left the house, and it seemed to upset you. Is there something you want to talk about?"

Cole looked at her, his smile disappearing. He moved his hand down to caress her neck. "It was from one of the network executives who's offered me a job. He's pressing me for a decision."

"Is that the reason you needed some privacy away from everything and everyone?"

"I have less than six weeks before I have to make a decision on whether or not to take a job as a sportscaster for one of the major networks. Actually two networks have made offers."

"Is that something you want to do?" she asked, noticing his lack of enthusiasm when he talked about such an important career opportunity.

He pulled her closer, placing his arm about her waist. "What I really want is to play baseball."

More than ever, Lucky wanted to comfort him, but held back for fear of insulting his male pride. She could and would have comforted Greg. He'd have wanted and needed her care. But Cole was so different from her late husband, so much stronger and harder. "It's not easy when our lives don't go as we planned."

"Yeah, well, taking the sportscasting job would mean a continuation of two things I've always enjoyed." When she looked at him questioningly, he grunted. "Big money and celebrity status."

"Those things are very important to you?" Lucky had never had either, and never wanted either. But she understood only too well what it was like to want to retain

something important, something that really mattered in
your life. Perhaps Holly House was to her what fame and
fortune were to Cole.

"I don't really need the money. I spent a lot the first few
years I played, then I got smart and started investing. And
even now, nearly two years after my accident, I find fans
wherever I go."

"Would you be happy as a sportscaster? You'd have to
stay on the road traveling all the time, wouldn't you?" A
feeling of loneliness washed over her as she thought about
never seeing Cole again except on television. She couldn't
allow this man to become important to her. She had already lost too much to risk losing again. But was she the
kind of woman who could settle for less than a commitment? Did she dare think about an affair?

"I really don't know what I want to do with the rest of
my life. The traveling has never bothered me because I'm
single."

"What if you got married someday?" She realized the
question was highly personal, even suggestive. She hoped
he wouldn't think she was referring to the two of them.
Marriage was too risky. Loving someone enough to com-
mit to a lifetime together meant taking a chance on losing
that person. Her life was filled with losses, starting with
her father's desertion and culminating with her beloved
grandmother's death last year. Loving meant losing, and
she'd lost all she intended to lose.

"I suppose a wife would travel with me," he said, looking across the lake. "I was engaged before the accident,
and my traveling didn't seem to bother Kristin."

Lucky had known, of course, that there had been a fiancée. Some tall, blond model. Uncle Pudge had told her
more about the situation than she'd wanted to hear. The
engagement had been broken a few months after Cole's

nearly fatal car crash. Lucky wondered who had ended the relationship. "Where is she now?"

"Who?"

"Kristin."

"Still modeling in New York."

"Do you ever see her? I mean, you must bump into her occasionally since you...well, I'm sure you still have friends in common. You probably attend the same parties, things like that." Lucky knew she was making a complete fool of herself, but she found it difficult to stop babbling.

Cole pulled her into his arms, his head descending, his lips covering hers so quickly she had no time to do anything but accept his kiss. She flung her arms around his neck and opened her mouth to his invasion. His tongue thrust into her, hot and furious. She moaned and clung to him with fierce possessiveness. No other woman mattered, she told herself. For now, Cole Kendrick was hers, and she had no intention of sharing him.

Cole circled her lips with the tip of his tongue, then tenderly dusted her face with feather-light kisses. "Kristin is a part of my past. She has absolutely nothing to do with you and me. You're the only woman I want. Do you understand?"

Lucky let her arms fall to his shoulders, her body snuggled intimately against his. "I know I have no right to be jealous. I have no claim on you. I—"

"It's all right. I'm jealous as hell myself."

"What?"

"I'm jealous of every man who looks at you, especially Brewster."

"Rich was my husband's best friend, and now he's my friend."

"But you were more than friends with your husband. I know it's ridiculous to be jealous of a dead man, but I am."

"Don't be jealous of Greg. He was...you're...the two of you are so different. I could never compare you."

"Would you laugh if I told you I'm even jealous of Holly House?"

"You can't be!" Lucky gasped, her big gray eyes widening in surprise. "But Holly House is—"

"Is something you love more than anything on earth. I'd say that was reason enough for jealousy."

"Holly House has belonged to my family for generations." Lucky was hesitant to reveal the complete truth about her financial problems. She decided it was time to take a giant step forward and trust Cole with her secret. "If I can't make a success of the antique-shop grand opening and the tours during the holidays, I could lose Holly House."

Cole grasped her upper arms in his big hands, shifting his body away from her. "How is that possible?"

Lucky cleared her throat and looked directly at him, her lower lip trembling slightly. "When Greg died, his insurance didn't cover all the bills. Granny took out a mortgage on Holly House to help me pay off my debts. I promised her that I'd never let the bank take her home."

"My God! Does Pudge know?"

"Pudge Prater is a retired lawyer who spent every dime he ever made. It would worry him needlessly if he knew, since there's nothing he can do to help. I have part of the next payment saved, but I'm counting on earning enough in the next few weeks to make up the difference. Then in the spring I can open the bed and breakfast. Where Holly House is located is a prime real-estate location. If I were to lose it, they'd tear down the old place and sell off the land."

"Would you let me help you?" he asked.

"No." She tried to smile, but couldn't quite manage to fake the emotion.

"Lucky, I could loan you the money."

"Absolutely not. Holly House isn't your concern. It's not your problem."

"I'm making it my problem," Cole said.

"We may become lovers, but…can't you see… If I were to take money from you—"

"A loan."

"Even a loan would make me feel as if you were paying for my services."

"Lucky…"

"Besides, if all else fails, I still have my backup plan."

"Dare I ask what it is?"

"I'll go to Atlantic City and use my incredible luck at card playing in one of the casinos."

Cole's arms tightened about her, then released her, his dark eyes glaring at her with a wildness that frightened her. "You damn well won't. You may have a knack for poker, but you've said yourself that you've never really gambled…that it's against your principles."

"It wouldn't really be gambling. I win most of the time."

"I won't allow you to do something so foolish." He simply couldn't understand why she wouldn't just take the money from him. Hell, he couldn't let her go to Atlantic City. Anything could happen to her there.

"You won't allow me?" Lucky jumped up off the bench, her gray eyes flashing silver fire. "It would be as a last resort. Only if I don't make enough during the holidays to cover the January mortgage."

"I hate the idea of you going to Atlantic City. You'd be like a lamb led to the slaughter. You'd lose every cent you take with you. And every man in the town would be hot on your trail.''

"Cole, it would be one time. And I would win. Besides, I'm a grown woman. I can take care of myself.''

"Why even think about that alternative when I could easily give you the money?''

"No. Anyway, I'm going to make enough with my antique-shop grand opening and the holiday tours.'' She touched the side of his face with gentle fingers. "Let's not argue about some hypothetical situation.''

Cole relaxed, took her caressing hand into his and held it to his lips. "It seems like the future is pretty uncertain for the both of us.'' He kissed her hand. They looked at each other and smiled. "Since you can't solve my problems and you won't let me solve yours, let's go for a ride.''

"A ride?''

"Show me around Colbert County. Uncle Pudge has been my tour guide through Lauderdale County for days now.''

"All right. We'll go to Cherokee and up the Natchez Trace and back to Florence.'' Lucky was glad Cole had chosen not to pursue their argument. Neither of them could win. She'd never been one to use her skills to win money, but if high-stakes gambling was the only way she could save Holly House, even Cole Kendrick's objections wouldn't stop her.

Cole drove up the long driveway and parked his car in front of Holly House. He took the keys out of the ignition and put them in his pocket. Then he leaned back in the low-slung seat, turned to Lucky and smiled. He didn't say anything. He simply looked.

Lucky laid her head back into the soft leather seat and closed her eyes. She wanted to sit quietly here alone with Cole in the intimate confines of his classic sports car. She didn't want to rush inside as if she couldn't wait to hop into bed with the man who freely admitted his primary objective was to make love to her.

She had never experienced anything like this before, this raging desire for a man she barely knew. Somehow it didn't seem to matter tonight. Nothing mattered except being with Cole, loving Cole, becoming one with him. He hadn't spoken of love, only desire, and in some insecure part of her heart, Lucky wondered if she dared to risk giving herself to a man who made no commitments.

She admitted that what she felt for Cole Kendrick was more than lust, more than sexual need. Somehow, against her will, she was falling in love for the second time in her life, and this time she wasn't betting on a sure thing. If she made love with Cole tonight, she risked a broken heart when he moved on and out of her life. And yet a brief affair was all she wanted, wasn't it? Even if she couldn't stop herself from loving him, she had no intention of allowing him to become a permanent part of her life. When she lost him, she'd be prepared. She had to accept the inevitable, as she had so many times before.

"You're awfully quiet," he said, reaching out to run a finger across her closed lips.

"I was thinking." She opened her eyes, seeing his shadowy outline in the darkness.

"About me, I hope." He teased her lips apart with his finger.

"As a matter of fact, I was." She opened her mouth and nipped on the tip of his index finger.

"Wondering what it's going to be like for us?" He touched her tongue. She responded, tasting, then pulling his finger farther into her mouth to suckle.

"Wondering if I've lost my mind. I don't do things like this. I've never let passion overrule my common sense."

Her body swayed toward his, the bulky console between them preventing a closer contact.

He groaned, and his big hand clasped the back of her neck, her silky curls caught beneath his fingers. "I want to hold you in my arms, to kiss the breath out of you, but not in this damn little car."

Lucky pulled away from him and opened the door. "Then let's go to the house."

They hurried out of the Corvette and came together on the sidewalk. With hands clasped tightly, they ran as fast as Cole's hampered gait would allow, stopping breathlessly on the front veranda.

Cole grabbed her, crushing her body into his. His head lowered. His mouth descended, and their lips met in a fevered kiss. He rammed his tongue into her open mouth, and she moaned as her lips closed about him, holding him captive, stroking his invading tongue with her own. His hands ran frantically up and down her back, finally clutching her hips, thrusting her against his aching desire.

"Inside," she whispered between frenzied kisses, her fingers wild in his hair, her breasts rubbing against his hard chest.

Cole pulled the keys out of his pocket and unlocked the front door while possessively holding Lucky about the waist. The door swung open, and he dragged her quickly inside the foyer. Lucky leaned back against the wall, pulling Cole with her. His body covered hers while his hungry lips found her neck.

"God, you taste good. I want to kiss you all over, every soft, satiny inch of you," he said, then ran his hands beneath her sweatshirt, covering her breasts, kneading gently.

"Oh, Cole," she sighed. "I want to touch you and taste you everywhere."

He unhooked the front closure of her bra, allowing her full breasts complete freedom. They fell into his waiting grasp. He squeezed. Lucky sighed. He pinched her nipples between thumbs and forefingers. Lucky moaned. He pulled her sweatshirt up, lowered his head and laved one peak while his finger teased the other. Lucky cried out.

"I want you. I want you now, Lucky. I can't wait." He lifted her into his arms. She threw her arms around his neck and buried her face in his shoulder, whispering his name over and over. A slight trace of cologne still lingered on his skin, blending with the earthy manliness that was Cole Kendrick's own unique smell.

She covered his neck and face with quick, eager kisses as he mounted the stairs slowly, telling her in a man's passionate words how desperately he wanted her and how he intended to assuage that longing.

The blood drummed in Lucky's ears, the hot, raging blood flowing through her veins. "My bedroom . . . there on . . . the right."

Cole kicked the half-closed door with his booted foot and carried her inside the dark room. From the dim light in the hallway, he was able to make out the location of her canopy bed. He dropped her onto its soft surface, immediately falling on top of her. His hands pinned hers above her head.

"The first time is going to be too fast to satisfy either of us, but I can't wait. I can't slow down. Do you understand, honey?"

"I don't want you to slow down. I want you just as much as you want me."

"You couldn't possibly," he said, then covered her mouth with his own.

Lucky struggled to free her hands, but he held her while his tongue lunged into her again and again. Finally her hands were freed when he grasped the hem of her sweatshirt and, lifting her slightly off the bed, pulled the garment over her head. Her breasts beckoned his attention. His hands covered them, massaged them, aroused their tips to readiness. While his mouth tugged on one begging nipple, his hand tugged at the zipper of her corduroy slacks.

Lucky inched her hands up underneath his sweatshirt, her fingers glorying in the feel of thick, curling hair. "Hurry, Cole, hurry. I ache with wanting you."

He lifted her hips, his big hands pulling on her slacks, his mouth feasting on her exposed stomach.

The shrill ring of the bedside telephone didn't quite register in either Cole's or Lucky's brain for several minutes until the insistent clamor wouldn't be silenced.

"The phone," she whimpered.

"Damn!"

Cole picked up the receiver and handed it to her, then fell to his knees on the floor.

"Hello. Yes, this is she. What? Oh, God, no. No!" Tears filled Lucky's eyes, and the phone fell from her numb fingers.

"Lucky, honey, what is it? What's wrong?"

"I have to go to the hospital." She sat up on the side of the bed. "Oh, Cole, he may be dying."

Six

Cole sat on the edge of the vinyl chair in the emergency room waiting area. He loosened his grip on the armrests and stood up abruptly. If Lucky didn't come out of the ladies' room in the next few minutes, he intended to go in and see about her. He knew she wanted a few minutes alone to wash her face and compose herself. The news that Joel Haney's drunken father had beaten him to unconsciousness was a fact Lucky Darnell couldn't handle in a calm manner. Cole realized that she was the type of woman who would have cared if the boy had been a stranger, but she loved Joel, and his welfare was a major consideration in her life.

After Lucky had taken the call from the emergency room receptionist, they'd dressed quickly and rushed to the hospital. Unfortunately they hadn't been allowed to see Joel because the doctors were examining him, doing tests and trying to save his life.

When a nurse told Lucky that the boy had not regained consciousness, she'd given in to tears, and, once started, she couldn't seem to stop crying. He'd tried to comfort her, holding her, reassuring her, even promising that he'd make sure Joel's father never hurt him again. That was when she'd insisted on calling Uncle Pudge, but Cole had persuaded her to wait until they'd heard good news. He didn't dare admit that the report could be anything else.

The ladies' room door opened, and Lucky walked out. Her hair hung free in a riot of red curls down past her shoulders. Her usually glowing complexion was pale except for red blotches around her eyes, which were slightly puffy. Her thick eyelashes were still damp with tears. In long, quick strides, Cole reached her and pulled her into his arms. She went into his embrace eagerly, laying her head against his chest.

"Come on, honey, let's go sit down." Cole led her to a nearby couch. He held her close, one arm draped about her shoulders, the other across her waist. She rested the back of her head against his chest, her cheek brushing his soft sweatshirt.

"Any news?" she asked, her voice a mere whisper.

"Brewster's here. He said to tell you not to worry, that everything possible is being done for Joel."

"Hmm . . . mmm," Lucky closed her eyes and took several deep breaths. "As soon as we know something, I'm going to call Uncle Pudge. We've got to get Joel away from that crazy man. There has to be a way. This isn't the first time he's hit Joel. I've tried to persuade Joel to let me help him. He's so protective of his father. I just don't understand why. Oh, Cole, if he should die . . ."

"Don't, honey, don't." Cole soothed her, his big hand moving from her waist to stroke up and down her arm. He'd noticed that she always babbled whenever she was nervous. He wanted to help her vent her frustration, but

was afraid if she continued talking excessively she might
become hysterical.

"Uncle Pudge has a lot of friends, other lawyers,
judges, state representatives. After tonight Joel will not be
living at home with a man like Ellis Haney." She clutched
at Cole's sweatshirt, her fingers nervously twisting the
cloth into a wad. "I don't understand why things like this
have to happen. Why can't God give us all perfect parents, parents who love us, stay with us, take care of us?"

Cole took her face in one big hand, and his heart lurched
at the agony etched plainly on her beautiful features. He
wanted to kiss away the fresh tears falling from her eyes,
wanted to stop her near-hysterical ranting. He kissed her
with lips as tender and compassionate as the emotions in
his heart. "Hush, darling. Don't do this to yourself."

Lucky sniffled, threw her arms around Cole and cried.

He held her while she wept, her soft body trembling
within his embrace. After several minutes, Lucky pulled
out of his arms and wiped her face with her hands. She
looked at Cole and tried to smile.

"I'm all right," she told him. "I'm so glad you're here."

"Me, too," he said, taking her hand into his, bringing
it to his lips for a gentle kiss.

No matter how hurt and worried Lucky was, Cole sym-
pathized with Joel on a personal level that she would never
be able to comprehend. He wondered what she'd think if
he told her more about his father. Travis Kendrick had
been a battle-scarred, embittered man who turned more
and more to the bottle after his wife's death. He had allowed Cole and Becky to fend for themselves when Cole
had been a boy and his sister not much more than a tod-
dler. Cole had got tough fast, but not fast enough to protect Becky before the damage was done.

"Cole?" Lucky reached up and touched his cheek with her fingertips, encountering a single thin trail of moisture.

He squeezed her hand, knowing that this night was bringing back so many memories, memories of both his unhappy childhood and the more-recent tragedy of his accident. "I asked about Joel's father."

"Who did you ask?" Lucky looked at him, fear and concern bright in her eyes.

"I asked the receptionist, but she didn't have any information, and suggested I speak with the emergency room guard."

"And?"

"He told me that the policeman who came in with the ambulance told him that Ellis Haney's in jail. The neighbors called the police when they heard a ruckus. And those same neighbors made sure that somebody called you."

"Thank God. Now if they'd only keep Ellis in jail and throw away the key." Lucky ran nervous fingers through her hair. "What's taking them so long? I wish Rich would come out and tell us something. He must know I'm half out of my mind."

"Try to relax." Cole wanted to walk through the closed doors into the examining room and demand information, to tell the doctors that his woman was dying slowly with worry. "If there's any justice in this world, Joel will be all right. And I promise you that if Pudge can't pull enough strings to get custody of Joel, I'll hire the best lawyers in the country."

"Oh, Cole." Lucky nibbled on her lower lip, trying to stop it from trembling. "Do you know that you're a very special man?"

"I'm not really." His gaze locked with hers for one endless moment, a feeling beyond lust or even love passing between them. "You make me special. You think I'm more than I am."

"Cole," she whispered, taking his big hand in both of hers and bringing it up to rub gently against her cheek.

"Ms. Darnell?" A heavyset blond nurse stood in the doorway.

Lucky jumped up, Cole right behind her as she rushed over to the smiling woman. "How is he? Is he all right?"

Cole put his arm around Lucky and felt the quiver of fear surge through her.

"Dr. Brewster said to tell you that he'll be out directly and explain everything."

Lucky sighed in exasperation, clenched her teeth and groaned. "Can't you tell me anything now?"

The nurse smiled again and patted Lucky on the arm. "The boy has regained consciousness. I'm afraid that's all I know."

Lucky swayed into Cole, a sense of relief washing over them both. "Come on, honey," Cole said. "Sit down and let me go get you some coffee or cola or something."

Lucky rubbed her hands together, clutching and releasing them over and over again as she walked away from Cole. He started to follow her, but decided to give her some breathing space. She continued to pace around the small waiting room.

"I hate hospitals," she said, stopping to lean wearily against the wall. "Greg was in and out of hospitals for two years."

Dear God, she's in pain, he thought. She's hurting, and I can't help her because the pain is a part of her past, a part of her life that can't be changed. He'd never known a woman like Lucky, a woman who brought out all the protective instincts in him. The only other person he'd ever felt the need to protect had been his sister. It was odd desiring a woman and wanting to protect her all at the same time.

He'd thought he loved Kristin, but what he'd felt for her was nothing compared to what he felt for Lucky Darnell.

"Why don't you go get us some coffee?" Lucky realized that in his own way Cole was hurting just as badly as she was. For some reason he felt empathy for Joel. Perhaps there was more in Cole's past than the tabloids had reported.

"I'll be back in a minute." He looked at her, smiling.

She returned the smile, her heart filled with love for him. She nodded affirmatively, then watched him walk out of the room.

Like heavy fog lifting to reveal bright sunshine, Lucky's troubled mind admitted that she loved Cole Kendrick. She loved him passionately, completely in a way she'd never known existed. What she'd felt for Greg Darnell had been different, a pale comparison. Lucky sobered at the thought, feelings of guilt rushing through her. No, she told herself, don't punish yourself because you love Cole with an intensity you never felt for Greg. When Greg was alive, you adored him, shared years of happiness with him, stood by and cared for him until the day he died.

Lucky despised the smells permeating the air around her, the uniquely antiseptic odor, the faintly medicinal aroma. She resisted the urge to run outside into the cool, fresh night air, to escape the noises, the hushed silences that she associated with endless days and nights of watching her husband die, inch by agonizing inch.

She didn't realize that her steps had led her to the emergency room entrance, that her feet had triggered the automatic opening device, until she heard Cole's voice behind her. "Honey, are you all right?"

Suddenly she felt the brisk November air touch her face, swirling around her, chilling her. She shuddered, hugged herself for warmth, then relaxed before turning to face

Cole. "Yes, I'm all right. My mind wandered." She reached out and took a foam cup from his hand.

"Bad memories?" he asked, taking her by the elbow to lead her back to the couch.

"Nightmares." She sat down. Clutching the cup in both hands, she took several sips.

"Yeah, I can imagine. I have some hospital nightmares myself." Cole placed his cup on the metal coffee table littered with magazines and newspapers.

"Did I tell you that Uncle Pudge taught me to play poker when I was only four?" she asked, wanting desperately to banish all thoughts of Greg's slow death.

"And just when did you become so proficient at the game that you acquired a nickname?" He leaned back and crossed his legs, facing her, but not touching her.

"Oh, I was a regular shark by the time I was six, much to Mother's and Granny's disapproval. They were very strict, very moral. To this day, I find it difficult to play for money. When Rich and Suzy join us for our weekly games, we always play for pennies. Pennies that belong to me before and after the games." It always amazed friends and acquaintances alike that she possessed an uncanny ability with cards, but refused to use her talent to play for high stakes. But if all her well-made plans failed, she'd have no other choice than to gamble, and gamble big, in order to save Holly House.

"If you go to Atlantic City, you'll lose everything. You may be lucky at penny-ante poker, but Atlantic City is the big time."

"There's no point in our discussing this. Even if I could make you believe that I always win at least seventy-five percent of the time, you'd still call it gambling."

"A lady like you has no business in a gambling casino."

Lucky wondered exactly what he meant by *a lady like her*. No doubt he meant someone as refined and dull as an antique dealer in a small Southern town. "Even my one big vice doesn't make me an exciting woman, does it?"

"You're the most exciting woman I've ever known." He placed his hand on her knee, squeezing, then turned his hand palm up.

She placed her hand in his, clutching it with a give-me-strength desperation. "I will not lose Holly House. I've lost too much already. There are times when a person, even a lady like me, will do whatever has to be done."

Cole knew that all Lucky's problems boiled down to one thing—the man she'd loved and lost, the man she'd seen die slowly and whose death had resulted in enormous debts. Her need to save Holly House was so interwoven with memories of her late husband that she'd never be free of him if she lost her grandmother's home. "Tell me about your husband."

"Greg had cancer. Bone cancer." She held Cole's hand, wanting to share the memories with him, but hurting as if the pain was fresh. "He died two years, two months and one day from the time it was diagnosed."

"There's no need for you to tell me, to put yourself through it all over again."

"Yes, there is." Still holding his hand, she laid her head against the back of the vinyl couch and closed her eyes. "Greg and I had so much in common. We liked all the same things, wanted the same things. It was the most natural thing in the world to fall in love and marry, and then open our own antique shop. You would have liked Greg. Everybody did."

"I'm sure he was a very special man if you loved him."

"We decided to wait for a few years before having children. We wanted to make a success of the business, to have time just for ourselves. We hadn't been married quite three years when he became sick."

"It must have been horrible for you. It hurts me to think about what you must have gone through."

"I watched the man I loved, along with all our hopes and dreams, die slowly, one day at a time." She turned to Cole, no tears in her eyes, her body begging for his comfort.

He put his arms around her, his lips brushing her forehead, spreading quick kisses over her skin, over her hair.

"When he died, it took all of his insurance to pay the bills. The doctors, the hospitals, the medicine. It wasn't enough." She opened her eyes and looked up at Cole. "When Granny mortgaged Holly House so I could pay all Greg's bills, I promised her that I'd never lose Holly House." She wanted him to understand what that old house, those scant twenty acres, meant to her. Holly House was far more than her heritage, than sweet memories of her childhood. Holly House was a promise, a vow to a woman who'd been her stability, her mainstay.

Cole wanted to take away Lucky's pain, to give her peace and joy and love. He'd make sure that she didn't lose Holly House, that nothing and no one ever caused her sorrow and pain. She was his, and he would take care of his own.

He held her securely, his big hands tenderly soothing her. He laid his head on top of hers where it nestled into his chest. She smelled of fresh air and sunshine, of flowery perfume and of him. He breathed in his own essence where it clung to her, his heart beating wildly at the thought of how close they'd come to making love tonight. He understood all too well, now, that having sex with Lucky would not be like anything he'd ever experienced. He'd never wanted a woman the way he wanted her, but more important, he'd never needed to give of himself the way he longed to give to her.

"I should call Uncle Pudge," she said, raising her head slightly. "Maybe he can go ahead and make a few phone calls tonight. Get things started. I want to make sure that when Joel leaves the hospital, he doesn't have to go home to that man."

"Maybe Ellis Haney will spend some time in jail. It'll be hard for Joel to charge his father with abuse, but it's something he'll have to do."

"Wait here for me," she said as she got up. "I'll be able to see from the phone over there, but you wait here just in case they call for me and I don't hear."

"Sure." He didn't take his eyes off her while she walked across the room.

When she reached the wall pay phone, she hesitated. "Cole, do you have a quarter?"

He pulled the loose change from his jeans pocket as he stood up. He crossed the room and handed the coin to her. "I could talk to Pudge, if you want me to."

"No. I'll be all right." She dropped the coin in the slot and dialed. "Cole."

"Huh?"

"Stay with me. Okay?"

He stood behind her, placing an arm around her waist. She leaned back into him as the phone began to ring. "Miss Winnie, this is Lucky. Please let me speak to Uncle Pudge."

Cole held her as she told her great-uncle the situation. He could guess the old man's reactions by Lucky's end of the conversation. Where had people such as Lucky and Pudge been when he and Becky had needed help so badly? He supposed it didn't matter anymore. They had survived. As soon as he'd been old enough to make his own way, he'd taken Becky and run, hiding out from the old man until he'd given up looking for them. His senior year at Stanford, his sister had called and told him the old man was dead.

Cole could still smell the odor of cheap whiskey and hear the violent curses his father had thrown at him. He could still feel the pounding of the old man's fists. He could still see Becky's battered body lying on the kitchen floor.

"Thanks, Uncle Pudge. I'll call back just as soon as I know anything for sure." She hung up the phone and turned into Cole's arms.

He kept his arms around her as he moved her to his side. "Let's walk around in here. I don't think I can sit back down." He knew the restlessness came from the vivid memories running riot in his mind.

"Cole?"

"Huh?"

"Tell me about it."

"About what?"

"I'm not being nosy."

He stopped them by the double windows and gazed out into the parking area behind the emergency room. "My father was a drunk just like Ellis Haney. There was never any money because he drank away his check every month. And when Becky and I were kids, he...he knocked us around."

"Oh, Cole. I was afraid that's what it was." She held on to him tightly, as if she could surround him with her love.

"As soon as I could make enough money for us to live, I took Becky and we ran away." His dark eyes continued to stare out the window, but what he saw was his sister's unmoving little body crumpled on the linoleum floor. "Once, when he had one of his drunken tirades, he almost killed Becky. She was only six years old." Cole pounded his fists against the window frame.

Lucky held him while guttural moans vibrated from his throat. "How is she now...your sister?"

"She isn't married. Has no intention of ever marrying and having a family. She doesn't even date much," Cole replied, stilling his hands and placing his head against the windowpane.

"She doesn't like men because of your father's abuse?"

"She's afraid of men, I think. Everybody except me. I can give her everything money can buy, but all my money can't erase her memories...her fears."

"Or yours, it would seem."

"I promise that, if I have to move heaven and earth, Joel won't go back to his father."

Lucky took Cole's face in her slender hands, pulling his head down to hers. She kissed him with love and tenderness.

"Lucky?" Richard Brewster stood a few feet away, his blue eyes filled with irritation.

"Oh, Rich, how is he?" she asked, stepping away from Cole to go toward Richard.

Cole didn't move. He felt as if his heart had stopped beating. What if the boy were dead? How could Lucky survive such news? She'd been through so much already, lost so many people she loved.

Richard reached out for Lucky, but suddenly let his hands drop to his sides. "He's conscious, and all his vital signs are good. We're having him moved to a room right now."

When Lucky stepped toward the swinging doors leading to the examining rooms, Richard placed a hand on her shoulder to stop her. "You can go up and see him as soon as they get him settled in a room."

"How serious are his injuries?" Lucky asked.

"He's badly bruised. Pretty much as if he'd been in a fistfight. He's got a broken nose and some cracked ribs. His wrist is broken."

"Oh, my God," Lucky cried, covering her mouth with her hand.

Cole moved forward and placed a protective arm about her shoulders.

"The boy's fortunate he isn't more seriously injured. It's obvious he took quite a beating," Rich said.

"Exactly what's the prognosis?" Cole asked.

Rich tensed visibly, and when he replied, he looked directly at Lucky. "He'll be fine. A few days in the hospital and a few days recuperating at home, and he should be able to go back to school in a week or so."

"He won't be going home," Lucky said. "Uncle Pudge is making some phone calls right now to have Joel placed in his custody."

"Do you think that's wise?" Rich asked, seeming not to notice Lucky's shocked reaction, her silent gasp. "I'm sure social services can handle the matter."

"We don't want social services to handle the matter," Cole said, stepping in front of Lucky, his overwhelming presence demanding Richard Brewster's full attention. "You've handled Joel's broken bones—how about leaving the rest to us?"

"Us?" Rich eyed the big man suspiciously, then cast his gaze on Lucky.

"I want to see Joel." Lucky refused to allow Rich to intimidate her or make her feel guilty for the apparent closeness between Cole and her.

"If you're so concerned with the boy, Kendrick, you might want to check with admitting and get him a better room. After all, medicaid doesn't pay for private accommodations." Rich glared at Cole, animosity evident in his words and look.

"I'll be glad to take responsibility for all Joel's bills," Cole said. "You call admissions and have his room changed."

"You're being rather extravagant just to impress Lucky, aren't you? Or do you think getting her in bed is worth any cost?" Rich flung out the words like a gauntlet, daring his opponent to pick it up.

Lucky grabbed Cole by the arm, her touch halting his furious reaction. "No, Cole."

Richard turned to the receptionist. "Check with admissions in about five minutes to find out Joel Haney's room number, and then inform Ms. Darnell."

Fifteen minutes later Lucky and Cole walked into Joel's attractive private room. A young nurse's aide hummed as she quickly arranged an extra blanket at the foot of the bed, double-checked the water pitcher and adjusted the lights.

Lucky caught her breath at her first glimpse of the boy's battered face, his lanky body lying so still on the pristine sheets. "Joel?"

"He's awake," the young woman said. "I'm afraid they couldn't give him anything for the pain because of the slight concussion."

Lucky stopped by the bedside. Cole stood directly behind her. "Hey, there. You're going to be all right." She paused for several seconds, waiting to see if he would respond. When he neither spoke nor moved, she continued. "Uncle Pudge is going to have you placed in his custody. You won't ever have to go back to your father. I promise."

When Joel still didn't respond, Lucky looked up at Cole, her sad, gray eyes beseeching his assistance.

"There's nothing you can do to help your father," Cole said, moving to stand beside Lucky. "I know how you feel, but believe me, it's too late to save him. You have to save yourself."

"How could you...know...how I feel?" Joel demanded, his voice harsh.

"Because my old man used to beat the hell out of my sister and me when he went on a binge." Cole looked down at the bruised and helpless boy. "You owe it to yourself to escape. Pudge and Lucky want to help you. So do I."

"Yeah, sure." Joel refused to look up at the two concerned adults.

"Would you like for me to stay here with you tonight?" Lucky asked, running her hand gently over the boy's arm.

"Thanks, Lucky, but I'd rather be alone. Besides, this place is crawling with nurses."

"I'd like to stay." She smiled when he finally looked at her.

"Really. I want to be alone. To think...to make some plans."

"But—" Lucky said, then hushed when Cole tugged on her arm.

"Come on, honey. Sometimes a man needs to be alone."

Lucky's gaze went from Cole to Joel, seeing the exchange of understanding that passed between them.

Cole took Lucky's arm and led her to the door. "We'll see you tomorrow," he told Joel as he ushered Lucky outside into the hall.

"You males," Lucky said, placing her hands on her hips. "I think I should stay here with him."

"Look, honey, he's in pain, physical and mental. He doesn't want you to see that. Can't you understand?"

"Oh. I guess I'll never understand the male psyche."

"There's nothing to understand. Sometimes, when a man is hurting the most, he wants to protect the people he loves from experiencing that pain with him. Joel will want and need you tomorrow, but not tonight.''

"But what if he gets sick.''

"If he needed someone to stay with him, they would have told us.''

"I give up!''

"Then let's go home.'' Cole put his arm around her as they walked to the elevator.

"I've got to call Uncle Pudge,'' Lucky said, suddenly remembering her uncle didn't know Joel was going to be all right.

"Call him when we get home.'' Cole pulled her into the elevator.

"I'll call him from one of the pay phones downstairs in the lobby.''

"Okay, honey, whatever you want.''

Seven

——

Lucky relaxed on the sofa in her cozy den. With knees bent and one leg tucked under the other, she cuddled into the back of the overstuffed softness as she watched Cole place an extra log on the fire. It had been a long, horrible night. She knew they were both tired and overwrought, but their nerves were too frazzled and their senses too alert to find any solace in sleep.

After she'd made the second phone call to Uncle Pudge, they'd left the hospital and come home to the quiet stillness, the comforting presence of Holly House. When she'd told Cole she knew she couldn't sleep, he'd insisted on staying up with her. She'd made no protest. She needed him.

While her gaze moved slowly over Cole's big, muscular body, the mantel clock chimed two, reminding her of how late it was. If she were a sensible woman, she'd go to her room and flee temptation. She and Cole had shared a

traumatic experience. They'd also opened their hearts to
each other and shared their painful pasts. Tonight they'd
forged a bond that wouldn't be broken easily. Their relationship had progressed beyond lust, beyond mere desire.
In some almost mystical way, she and Cole Kendrick were
joined spiritually, and she understood in her heart of
hearts, it was the right time for them to join physically.

"Sure you don't want a brandy?" Cole asked as he sat
beside her on the couch, crossing his long legs at the ankles. "Or I could make some coffee or hot chocolate."

"No, I'm fine, really. I don't want anything to drink."

"Are you hungry? I could fix some sandwiches." He
couldn't bear to see her looking so forlorn, so unhappy. He
wanted to hold her, to love her, but she was so vulnerable
right now, he'd feel like a jerk if he took advantage of the
situation.

"All I need is you, Cole, here with me. I didn't realize
how badly I've missed having someone to share things
with, the good times and the bad." She wanted to reach
out, to touch him, for him to respond.

"I'm here, honey. Just tell me how I can help."

"I think I'd like to talk a little about Joel and about my
feelings, and even about Greg." She looked at Cole with
clear, dry eyes that pleaded for him to hold her.

"I'm a good listener," he said, tentatively touching the
side of her neck with his fingertips.

She leaned her head over to touch his hand. "Would you
hold me while we talk?"

Cole thought he would die of pleasure at her whispered
request. There was nothing on earth he wanted more than
to hold her, love her, cherish her. Tonight. Forever.
"Come here."

When he opened his arms, she moved into them, allowing him to adjust their bodies so that her back lay against
his chest, her head nestled at the curve of his shoulder, her

hips snuggled against his groin. "Now, talk," he said, his lips so close to her ear she could feel the warmth of his breath.

"Uncle Pudge said he…he's almost certain that he can have Joel placed in his custody. Joel could have a father and grandfather all rolled into one. Uncle Pudge would have made a fantastic father. In a way, he's the only father I've ever known."

"Don't you ever see your father?"

"My parents' divorce was very bitter. There was another woman involved. A woman who was pregnant with my father's child. Oh, Cole, I don't want or need to talk about this."

Sensing Lucky's bitterness toward her father, Cole knew that, like his relationship with his father, it was something best left alone. Some things you can't change no matter how much you'd like to. "Why didn't Pudge ever marry?" Cole asked, deciding to change the subject.

"He was in love with Miss Winnie, but he was a regular young rake. He broke hearts all over the state. When she would have married him, he wasn't ready to settle down. When he was ready, she was married to his best friend."

"Damn. They sure made a mess of their lives, didn't they?" If he loved a woman, he wouldn't wait around until he lost her to another man. A lifetime with the right woman was worth any sacrifice. Cole shook his head, shocked by his own thoughts. Being around Lucky Darnell was doing strange things to his powers of reasoning.

"They've been dating for the past ten years, since Miss Winnie's husband died. But she won't agree to marry him. I used to think it was a subtle form of revenge, but now I'm not so sure." Lucky felt Cole's arms cross over her waist, one hand tenderly caressing her stomach while the other lay unmoving below her breasts.

"It seems so unfair that they've probably loved each other all these years, and yet they'll never be husband and wife." Cole hadn't realized that people could actually love each other that much or for that long. He'd loved Kristin Taylor and had expected a busy and exciting life for the two of them. But their love had been shallow, based on good sex, good times and mutual enjoyment of the same life-style. Now a marriage based on anything except a for-ever-after kind of love repulsed him. He supposed it was only natural for a man's values to change as he grew older. Or maybe they changed when he met a special woman who made him think of the future.

"I do believe you have a romantic soul, Cole Kendrick."

He laughed at the thought. He wasn't a romantic. He was a hard-nosed realist. But perhaps he was changing. He had to admit he'd never courted a woman. And never had he waited so long to bed a woman he desired.

"Yes, you, Cole Younger Kendrick." She turned her body slightly so she could look up at him.

"God, how I've hated that name. My old man had a real sense of humor, didn't he? How many men name their sons after a notorious outlaw?"

"I love your name," she said, then kissed him squarely on the chin.

"Don't start anything you don't intend to finish, Lucille Leticia Llewellyn Darnell."

"Oh! Who told you? I'll kill Pudge Prater." Lucky jerked away, sitting up straight, her gray eyes flashing.

Cole pulled her back into his arms and held her tightly as she squirmed, trying to free herself. "Honey, if you don't quit rubbing against me like that, I won't be responsible for what comes up."

Lucky continued to move for several seconds until the meaning of his words sank in. She laughed, then deliberately moved her hips against his aroused body. "It's too late—the damage has already been done."

"What do you intend to do about it, Lucky Lu?" The lower part of his body surged upward, making her even more aware of his readiness.

Lucky licked her lips with the tip of her tongue as she smiled up at him, a come-hither gleam in her eyes.

"I'm not exactly sure how to handle this situation, that is if you are expecting me to handle it." Her lips curved into an even more provocative smile. "It might take a considerable amount of thought to make such an important decision."

"Would you allow me to make a few suggestions?" he asked, his face somber, but devilment twinkling in his dark eyes.

"Oh, yes, I'm always open to the right suggestions." She placed her hand over his where it rested beneath her breast, lifted it and laid it over her heart.

"Lucky, I can give you what you're asking for," he told her, his open palm covering her breast, squeezing gently. "But I want you to be damn sure it's what you want. You've made it plain since we first met that you're not the type of woman for brief affairs. Tonight you're vulnerable. You've been through an emotional wringer."

She placed two fingers on his lips. "Hush. I know what I said, how I've always felt. But...I want you, Cole. I...I need you."

"Are you sure, honey? Because once I start, I don't intend to stop until we're both out of our minds with pleasure, and then I intend to start all over again."

"Why don't you stop talking, Cole Kendrick, and give me some of that pleasure now." She turned in his arms, the side of her body pressing against his arousal, the edge of one breast crushed against his chest.

Cole pulled her onto his lap where she was half sitting, half lying on him. "I want to do things with you I've never wanted to do with other women," he groaned as she threw her arms around his neck.

Her lips met his in an urgent kiss, a kiss of passion and need too long denied. His lips covered hers in moist abandon, his tongue driving into her with a savagery neither had ever known. His big hands moved over her in a frenzy of exploration, stopping to cup the fullness of her derriere, urging her into the juncture between his thighs.

Lucky kissed with the same wildness, the same hungry need, her tongue battling, then mating with his as one kiss progressed smoothly into another. She clutched at his broad shoulders, kneading the soft sweatshirt and the hard muscles beneath. When his tongue moved outside and he nibbled on her tender lips, she whimpered, running her hands between them, tugging at his clothing.

"You want to touch me, honey?" he asked, his mouth against hers. His tongue traced the outline of her lips. "Here, I'll help you." He released her long enough to pull his sweatshirt over his head and toss it onto the floor.

Lucky looked at his naked chest gleaming like pure gold in the firelight, the mass of dark chest hair a seduction her fingers could not resist. She touched him hesitantly at first, running her fingertips lightly over his body. "Oh, Cole, I love to look at you, to touch you."

"Then don't stop. Keep touching me." He made no move to touch her while she caressed him, her fingers playing through his hair, her nails scraping his hardened nipples. "Oh, God, woman, your hands feel so good on my body."

Her trembling fingers edged downward, stopping at his belt. She looked questioningly into his loving eyes and saw acquiescence. She unbuckled his belt and unsnapped his jeans.

"I want it, honey. I want you to take me in your hand and love me, but if you do, I'll explode. I've got to slow down."

Her fingers moved up and down the zipper. She wanted to remove the rest of his clothes, to see him completely naked, to touch him and love him with her hands and mouth. "I want to touch you so badly," she mumbled, burying her face in his chest, her nose nuzzling, her tongue flicking across his nipples.

"I want that, too, but just not right now." He grabbed the edge of her sweatshirt, slowly pulling it up her body, over her breasts, over her head. He tossed it on the floor beside his. He released the hook on her bra and gently lowered the lacy garment. Her breasts swelled in response to his predatory gaze.

Lucky saw a look of pure hunger and loving adoration in his compelling brown eyes. She closed her eyes, sighing when his hands lifted her breasts, his thumbs flicking her nipples. "Ahh...ahh...yes..."

He had never seen anything as beautiful as Lucky with her breasts bared, her ivory complexion flushed, her eyes closed as she moaned with pleasure. "I want to put my mouth on your breasts, to taste your sweetness."

She opened her eyes just in time to see his head descend. His open mouth suckled her while his finger and thumb gently pinched the erect nipple of her other breast. It was the most agonizing pleasure she'd ever known. She wanted to beg him to stop, and she wanted to beg him for more. Yearning, so intense she thought she'd die, coursed from her heavy breasts to the essence of her being. Her body cried for fulfillment.

"This won't be just sex," Cole growled, his big hands working at the snap of her slacks, then deftly lowering the zipper. "I want us to make love, honey."

Lucky lifted her hips, helping him remove her slacks and panties in one swift movement. "I want that, too," she said, delighting in the look of wild longing she saw in his eyes.

He planted blissfully light kisses across her shoulders as he turned her, allowing her to fall along the length of the couch. He shed his jeans and briefs, kicking them away while his mouth lowered to her stomach, his tongue drawing circles on her soft flesh. "I don't think I'll ever be able to get enough of you."

"I know. I know," she said, her body bucking upward when his mouth lowered, brushing her intimately.

"Oh, Lucky, honey, I can't wait. Forgive me." He moved up and over her, his tongue gliding over her satiny-smooth skin. He spread her legs with his knee and lowered himself between her open thighs.

She felt the steely heat of his arousal against her femininity. She ached with the need to sheath him, to consume his strength, to claim his masculinity. "Now, now," she cried.

"Hard and fast...slower next time...promise..." His words were lost as his mouth consumed hers, his tongue plunging as his manhood drove into her waiting body. With fast, hard thrusting movements, he conquered her body. With frenzied counter moves, Lucky succumbed to the ecstatic pleasure building within her.

Their sweat-slick bodies moved in animalistic abandon. They were totally lost in passion. Unbearable tension built within them as their movements became more frantic. With one final push, Cole trembled with release, a cry of manly exhilaration echoing in the quiet room. Lucky felt the explosion beginning and clung to his sweat-dampened back, arching herself into him for the final stroke that sent her over the edge into mindless oblivion.

They lay in each other's arms, their naked bodies luxu-riating in the sexual moistness. He shifted his body so that he lay wedged beside her on the sofa. One big hand ca-ressed her neck and cheek, turning her face into his kiss. A sweet, sweet aftermath of loving, the kiss was as pa-tiently tender as the loving had been frantically savage.

"Lucky," he whispered. "Oh, God, lady, you're won-derful."

"You're pretty wonderful yourself," she said, glorying in the feel of his huge body nestled against her. "I've never...it was so..." She ran loving fingers across his chest, curling his dark hair around them.

"I think this was a first for both of us. I've never wanted anything so much, never enjoyed anything so much."

"It's never been like this before." Lucky knew that this was the time for truth. She wanted desperately to tell him she loved him, that she wanted a lifetime of loving and caring.

"You're mine now, lady. You know that, don't you?" He clutched her hip, squeezing, the gesture one of owner-ship.

"That works both ways. You belong to me now, Cole Kendrick, and I'm a woman who will not share." She reached out and clutched his hip, squeezing.

Deep, soul-happy laughter shook his body as he gath-ered her into his arms and kissed her soundly. "Well, since we've got that settled, I think it's time to move along to act two." He shoved her upward, his own naked body follow-ing until they sat upright on the sofa.

"Act two?" She moved over him, her naked body scrubbing across his hairy legs as she stood up.

"Just where do you think you're going?" He stood up behind her and grabbed her wrist, pulling her into his em-brace.

She ran her hands over his arms, fondling the sinewy
strength of his biceps. "All that exercise made me hungry. I thought I'd see what I could find in the kitchen."

"I'm hungry, too," he said, taking her buttocks in his
big hands, bringing her downy softness to his bulging
hardness.

"Cole?" Her body moved instinctively against him,
sighing with her own renewed desire.

"Let's feed our hunger in here instead of the kitchen."
One of his big hands soothed and petted up and down her
hip while the other hand covered her breast, repeatedly
kneading its fleshy weight. "I'm going to lay you down in
front of the fire and look at every inch of your body. And
when I finish looking, I'm going to touch you . . .
everywhere."

She clung to him as he walked her near the fireplace and
slowly lowered them both to their knees.

"You're such a beautiful man," she said. From high
cheekbones to muscular thighs, Lucky's hands paid tribute to his masculine body. Her fingers hesitated at the
thick, rough scars covering his left hip and thigh.

"Not pretty, is it?" He pulled her hand away from his
scarred flesh.

She jerked her hand free from his hold, then let her fingers explore his old wounds with the healing touch of a
woman's love. "You're beautiful. All of you. These scars
are just a part of the man you are now. They're not ugly.
Nothing about you is ugly."

"You really mean that don't you, honey?" He saw the
look of love in her eyes and wondered if he dared believe
what he saw. Why did it matter so much if she loved him
or not? Why was it so important that she be able to accept
him exactly the way he was?

"Oh, Cole, don't you know how special you are?"
Lucky lay down on the soft cotton rug in front of the

glowing fire, her arms extended outward, inviting the man she loved into her embrace.

Cole took both her hands in his, lowering his mouth to kiss the tips of all ten fingers, slowly lingering over each one. "You make me special, Lucky. You make me feel like a man wants to feel."

"Then it's a mutual feeling, because I've never felt more womanly, more purely female in all my life." She closed her eyes in anticipation as his hairy knee parted her thighs. Her mouth opened as a tinge of forthcoming pleasures rippled through her.

Cole, still on his knees, looked down at her, creamy warm and satiny smooth. The firelight cast soft shadows across her beautiful face and gloriously naked body, turning her fair, flawless complexion to gold-dusted ivory. Reaching down, he braced himself above her with one muscular arm placed on the floor while the other began an exploration of her neck and shoulders. His body touched hers intimately, his maleness throbbing against her.

"I want to touch you all over," he said while his hands did just that. As he worked his way down her body, he lay beside her, keeping one leg wedged between her thighs until his hands reached lower and lower. He slid his body down her as his hands caressed her knees, her calves, her ankles and her feet.

He lifted one small foot, his fingertips running sensuously up and down each toe. "You're beautiful everywhere."

His mouth began a moist journey from her ankles to the insides of her thighs. Lucky lay quivering, her hands clutching his head when his tongue went into play. "Cole...Cole..."

His mouth moved upward, across her flat stomach and waist, up to her breasts. "You taste so good, honey. So good...so good..."

His lips covered the tip of one breast, and a fierce hunger to be inside her rushed through him. He massaged her other breast, paying particular attention to the turgid nipple. Once again Cole parted her thighs, the feel of her silky flesh driving him crazy. She tasted like woman; she smelled like woman, pure, sweet, hot female ready to mate. He rubbed against her. She arched her hips. His mouth covered hers as he entered her with one swift thrust.

Lucky moaned into his mouth, delighting in the feel of his tongue and his manhood impaling her simultaneously. She felt consumed by this man, absorbed into him. A joining so complete that neither knew where one began and the other ended. They were one in every way a man and woman can be.

Cole growled as he surged himself in and out of the willing woman lying beneath him. Lucky clung to him, moving passionately to the ancient rhythm programmed into her femininity. A rhythm as old as mankind. Cole's mouth moved from one breast to the other, drawing on her, increasing her desire until the frenzy within them reached the point of no return. Cole moved harder and faster, sweat coating his body, his big hands urgently lifting her hips for the final thrust that carried Lucky over the top. Her hot, damp body trembled with a release so strong she thought she was dying with pleasure. Cole allowed her body time to reap the full benefits before he drove into her harder and harder until his own release came.

His groans were animalistic male sounds, primitive and untamed. He tried to speak, to tell her how he felt, but there were no words for feelings beyond ecstasy.

He didn't know how long they lay together, side by side, arms about each other. Their hearts beat erratically, and their lips played games, their fingers lazily exploring in the soft, sweet aftermath. He realized they couldn't stay in the den, naked and uncovered the rest of the night.

"Let's go to bed, honey," he said, pulling her to her feet, holding her close.

"My room," she whispered, nuzzling his neck. "I feel as if I could sleep a thousand years."

Cole chuckled as he led her out into the hall and up the stairs.

Sleep was something that had to wait for Lucky until well after dawn because she found Cole an insatiable lover, much to her delight. Each time was full and rich and complete, surprising them both. Even the merest touch was pleasure, the slightest brush of the lips a joy. She was sure no two people had ever loved the way they did, had ever felt such complete, soul-binding rapture.

Finally, when the sky was streaked with colorful hues of a new morning, Lucky and Cole slept, sated and peaceful. Their naked bodies lay entwined on the enormous four-poster bed where several generations of Prater women had conceived and later given birth.

Lucky opened her eyes, her lids heavy from sleep. She reached out to touch Cole, but found the bed empty of another body. Her hand ran over the sheets where he had lain, his warmth still in them. She pulled his pillow into her arms, breathing the smell of his masculine aroma. A smile of utter contentment curled her love-swollen lips. She ran her tongue over them, remembering the countless passionate kisses she'd shared with Cole. The very thought warmed her body, tensing her inside. She couldn't believe that her body still hungered for his when she'd made a glutton of herself on him for endless hours.

For several minutes she simply luxuriated in the bed, stretching her body, loving every sore muscle that bore witness to the pleasures she'd known with such a virile man. She wondered why Cole had left her bed, wondered

where he was. She looked at the alarm clock on the bedside table. It was past nine o'clock, and she'd overslept.
She'd given no thought to setting the alarm, but it really
didn't matter. This wonderful union between her and Cole
was far too wonderful and much too important to worry
about anything else.

She got up, found her housecoat in the closet and
slipped on her fuzzy slippers. Surely Cole was downstairs
somewhere. Or perhaps he'd gone for an early morning
walk around the grounds. Maybe he had some thinking to
do about last night. Wherever he was, and for whatever
reason he'd left without awakening her, she didn't care.
She'd find him and tell him she loved him and wanted to
be with him forever. She'd wanted to cry out her love every
time he'd taken her, every time fulfillment had claimed her,
but she'd held back because she'd wanted to hear the
words from him first. He hadn't said them. He'd said
everything else a woman could possibly want to hear,
stirred her to passion with his compliments and praise, but
not once had he said, "I love you."

As Lucky went down the back stairs, she suddenly remembered that today was the day the ladies from the genealogical society were supposed to meet at Holly House
and plan their monthly meeting. She had promised them
she'd take at least thirty minutes from her busy schedule
to meet with them. It was simply too late to call and cancel now. She'd have to make coffee and run down to the
Quick-Mart for fresh doughnuts. There wouldn't be time
to do anything else. She'd wanted to ask Cole to spend the
day with her, to help her, and perhaps teach him something about antiques.

When she reached the bottom of the stairs, she heard
Cole's deep voice coming from the kitchen and wondered
if Uncle Pudge was already home. Just as her hand reached

out for the doorknob, she heard Cole say, "No, Kristin, I
don't want you to do that."

Lucky's whole body stiffened. Kristin? Dear God, not
Kristin Taylor, his ex-fiancée, she prayed silently.

Lucky didn't care if she was eavesdropping. She had to
know who Cole was talking to and why. Could he have
called the woman? She hadn't heard the phone ring, but
then she'd been fast asleep. The jealous beast within her
demanded that she rush into the kitchen, grab the phone
out of Cole's hand and tell the woman on the other end
that Cole Kendrick was off-limits. She wanted this ex-
fiancée to know that she no longer had any claim on him,
that Cole was the personal property of Lucky Darnell now
and forever. But the more sensible woman inside Lucky
forced her to stand quietly at the closed door, listening and
waiting.

Cole spoke so softly that Lucky couldn't make out
everything he said. A muffled word now and then. Sometimes entire sentences when he raised his voice as he'd done
earlier. Flashes of a tall, bosomy blonde went through
Lucky's mind. She vaguely remembered Uncle Pudge
showing her tabloid pictures of Cole and the "voluptuous
model" to whom he was engaged. Intense jealousy ripped
through Lucky. She couldn't bear the thought that Cole
had loved another woman, that Kristin Taylor had known
the heat of Cole's passion.

"No, Kristin, don't come down here!" Cole shouted.

Lucky couldn't make out anything else he said because
his voice had returned to normal. Finally she heard Cole
hang up the phone and shuffle around in the kitchen. She
made no move to enter the room. She couldn't storm in
there and demand a reason for his conversation. Cole had
made her no promises, she reminded herself. He hadn't
even professed to love her. Despite his claim of possession
and her counter claim, she didn't have any rights where he

was concerned. She wasn't his wife or even his fiancée. She was simply his lover.

Her hand shook when she clutched the doorknob. She opened the door and walked into the kitchen, willing herself to stay calm.

Cole saw her and smiled, his eyes running over her from head to toe with a loving affection. "Well, good morning, beautiful."

"Morning." She forced a smile, her heart hammering wildly in her chest, the pain of uncertainty stabbing her repeatedly.

He pulled her into his arms and kissed her tenderly. "Mmm...mmm. You're still warm and sweet."

She put her arms around his waist and held him, the embrace a balm to the ache inside her. "How long have you been up?"

"About thirty minutes," he said, then kissed her on the neck. "I took a shower, shaved and changed clothes. I thought I'd put on some coffee and bring it up to you."

"I can make coffee." What else did you do? she wanted to scream. Did you call Kristin Taylor? Why would you want to talk to your ex-fiancée after what we shared?

"Why don't I make the coffee, and you scramble us some eggs?" He turned her around and swatted her behind. "Get with it, woman."

Lucky tried to respond normally, as if she hadn't overheard his telephone conversation, as if she didn't want to ask him a dozen questions. "You men!" She tried to sound teasing. "You always want your pleasure immediately."

"You bet," he said, winking at her.

Before Lucky could open the refrigerator, the phone rang. She hesitated picking up the receiver. What if Kristin Taylor was calling him back? Drawing on reserved strength, she answered the phone, relieved when she heard

Beatrice Lewis's voice. "No, Beatrice, I haven't forgotten. Yes, I promise you all at least thirty minutes. No. It's all right. I'll see you around eleven. Bye."

"Who was that?" Cole asked.

"The vice president of the genealogical society I belong to. We're having a short meeting here at the house today."

Lucky took a carton of eggs from the refrigerator.

"I was hoping we could spend the day together," he said.

"Why don't you do your own thing this morning, and then this afternoon I'll give you a tour of the rooms I'm converting into an antique shop?"

"After breakfast could I persuade you to spend some time with me?"

Lucky looked across the room at him. He stood by the nineteenth-century pie safe, his dark eyes sparkling, his mouth intimating a smile.

"Cole, I . . . I have so much to do." She wanted him to tell her about the phone call. It stood between them like an invisible barrier, one he didn't even realize was there.

"I'll help you this afternoon and tonight. We'll catch up on whatever you get behind with."

"If we hurry with breakfast, we should have an hour before I have to get ready for Beatrice and the other ladies." She opened the egg carton and took out four eggs.

"Forget the scrambled eggs. Let's have coffee and toast. That'll give us a few extra minutes." He laughed as he came over to her, hugging her, running his big hands up and down the sides of her body.

"Make the coffee." The words came out quickly, her breath catching in her throat when his hands covered her breasts.

He squeezed her lovingly, then released her and obeyed her command to make coffee. "Later?"

"Later." There was no doubt in her mind that she would follow him up the stairs and back to bed as soon as they finished their hurried breakfast. She knew she would make love with him, finding mindless pleasure in his arms. She doubted she would ever be able to resist him again. But she couldn't forget his phone call or the fact that he hadn't mentioned it to her.

In a couple of weeks he'd be going to New York. Would he see Kristin Taylor? If the phone call had been innocent, meaningless, why hadn't he told her? she wondered. Did he still love his ex-fiancée? When he went to New York, would he stay with the other woman? Share her bed?

Lucky choked back the tears building inside her. No, dammit! In the weeks she had left with Cole, she would love him so fiercely, give him so much of herself, that nothing and no one would be able to take him from her. Somehow, someway, she intended to keep the man she loved. She wasn't going to lose—not this time.

Eight

The sound of crunching leaves echoed in Lucky's ears as she walked along the banks of Cypress Creek. She could hear Cole's laughter and see the triumphant look on his face as he reeled in another catfish. She decided it was time to start cleaning their catch if they intended to eat before dark.

Reluctantly she had agreed to this fishing jaunt. She hated leaving Joel. Thank God, Uncle Pudge had been able to pull a few strings and have Joel placed in his custody. If everything went as planned, Joel would become a permanent part of their family. And, she had to admit, she wanted and needed Cole to be a part of that family, too. The man and boy had grown closer in the two days since Joel's release from the hospital. She knew Cole could understand and help Joel in ways she never would be able to.

Knowing that she'd left Joel in Uncle Pudge's and Suzy's loving care allowed her to enjoy this afternoon. Cole had reminded her that, in the past four days since he'd been working day and night to help her with Holly House Antiques, she was ahead of her self-imposed schedule. But she was here mainly because she couldn't resist Cole's charm. For the past ninety-six hours, she and Cole had been practically inseparable. They'd even bathed together, and she'd never done that before, not even with Greg. But she had stopped comparing Cole to her dead husband. They were totally different men, and the love she felt for Cole was completely different from what she'd felt for Greg. Occasionally she felt a twinge of guilt for loving Cole so passionately, but she forced those negative feelings aside. Her greatest concern was losing him.

Lucky walked up the hill, set the fishing bucket on the picnic table, reached inside and carefully removed the fish. She placed it on the wooden block and severed its head, then adeptly filleted it. She followed the same procedure with the rest of their catch before starting a fire in the open grill.

She liked her cousin Nan's home here at the edge of the creek, the property consisting of ten acres of cleared and wooded land. She certainly appreciated having relatives who could provide her with access to her favorite sport.

Lucky loved autumn, the cool bright days and chilly nights. She savored the colors and sensations unique to the season. For her, there was a peace about this time of the year, a sense of coziness. And Lucky liked coziness—in her home and in her life. It was strange that she could feel cozy with a man like Cole Kendrick. She wondered whether or not he'd laugh if she told him. He was a man who'd never had a home, who was as restless and free as the wind. Would he balk and run when she revealed more of her nesting instincts? Those instincts were a vital part of who and what Lucky Darnell was. She was a woman who wanted a home and a family. She didn't long for big-city lights and excitement.

Lucky arranged the catfish in the pan and placed them over the fire, then removed the contents of the large picnic basket and placed the items on the table.

"Hey, come give me a hand." she called out to Cole. "It's after four."

"We can eat in the dark," he said, obviously not ready to stop fishing.

"Just for that remark, you can come on right now and finish frying these fish."

Cole grinned and shook his head. "That's woman's work."

Lucky glared at him, a mock frown on her face. "Chauvinist!"

"Yep." Still smiling, Cole pulled in his empty line, gathered up his equipment and walked up the hill toward Lucky.

Forty-five minutes later darkness surrounded them while they sat at the picnic table listening to the hushed clamor of nighttime by the water.

Cole stood and pulled Lucky to her feet, putting an arm around her waist. "Let's take a walk and work off some of that food."

"Good idea."

Only the moonlight allowed them to see the path leading into the woods. Neither of them spoke; each simply enjoyed the presence of the other. There was so much between them that had been left unsaid, Cole thought, as he made his way slowly, carefully beside the woman who was becoming the most important thing in his life—too important for a brief love affair. It's a wonderful feeling, he decided as he looked over in the darkness at his beautiful Lucky, his warm and passionate lover. It's wonderful and it's scary to care so much about another human being. His feelings for Lucky were so different from anything he'd ever felt. If he asked Lucille Leticia Llewellyn Darnell to leave Holly House and go with him to New York, would she? he wondered. Did he dare hope he meant that much to her?

Cole reached out for Lucky's hand, but his foot jabbed into a tree root concealed by fallen leaves, He moved too quickly trying to balance himself, and his bad leg bolted. He reached out, breaking his fall by taking hold of a nearby tree. "Damn!"

"Cole, are you all right?" Lucky didn't know exactly what had happened, only that Cole had almost fallen.

"I forget I don't have two good legs anymore." He hated to appear less than perfect, less than one-hundred percent whole in front of his woman.

When she reached out to help him, he shrugged her hands off and leaned back against the tree trunk. "I'm okay. I didn't fall. I'm not a total cripple."

Lucky's spine stiffened. "Don't ever use that word to describe yourself," she told him. "When you say it, it's filled with self-hate and pity."

"If I didn't have this crippled leg, I'd still be playing baseball."

"My God, Cole, can't you be grateful that you weren't killed in that wreck instead of bemoaning the loss of your career?"

"My career was my life." He stepped away from the tree and stood directly in front of her. "Can't you understand? Baseball made me who I was. I was nothing, nobody, before baseball."

Lucky took one of his big hands into hers. "Is that what's wrong? Do you think that without a baseball career you'll be nobody again?"

For a long time he didn't reply. He stood in the darkness, holding her hand, his breathing deep and labored as if he were fighting a battle within himself. "Cole Kendrick is a celebrity athlete, a stud with the ladies and a star on the field."

Lucky ached inside, feeling the pain he felt, knowing the loneliness and vulnerability he tried so hard to hide. She wanted to tell him that he didn't have to be a tower of macho strength all the time—that with her he could ask and be given comfort and support. But would, could, a man like Cole trust her enough to admit his weaknesses?

"Say something, dammit!" He released her hand, but didn't move away from her.

"What do you want me to say? Yes, I know you were the biggest name in baseball a couple of years ago. Yes, I know that every woman in the world fantasized about being your lover. Yes, I know you've been with more women than you can remember. Yes, I know that I'm just one more..." She couldn't bear being near him another minute. Tears filled her eyes. She turned and walked away, her steps quickening when she heard him moving behind her.

"Lucky?" When she didn't stop or reply, he moved faster and called her name again. "Lucky?"

"Leave me alone." She struggled when his arms surrounded her, turning her to face him. "No, Cole, I—"

He didn't give her a chance to protest further. He lowered his head and took her mouth in a kiss that said everything he couldn't put into words. His tongue thrust into her, his big hands pressed her against him as if he were trying to fuse them into one being. The kiss went on and on. Lucky melted, her resistance disappearing like a puff of smoke in the wind. She clung to him, her lips and tongue responding in a frenzy of passion.

She broke the kiss when Cole slipped one hand beneath her sweater to fondle her breast. "No, Cole, please stop."

His hand stilled on her breast while his lips hovered above hers. "Lucky, sweet, beautiful Lucky. Don't ever compare yourself to any other woman I've known. And never, never think that you're simply one more in a long line of females."

Lucky closed her mouth tightly, salty tears clogging her throat. She tried to speak, to tell him why she felt the way she did, but the words wouldn't come without the tears, so she remained silent.

"Lucky, you're special," Cole said, then bestowed a series of quick, adoring kisses all over her face. "I've never cared about anyone the way I care about you. You've brought out a part of me that I didn't know existed. Somehow you've managed to touch my soul."

"Oh, Cole." She wanted to believe him. She had to believe him, because she felt exactly the same way. He had brought to life within her a savagely passionate woman who wanted to stake her claim and threaten death to any other female foolish enough to try to take Cole from her.

"I know it isn't going to be easy for us, honey. I know I'm probably the wrong kind of man for you. But when I go to New York, I don't want it to be the end of us. I want...I want more for us." He removed his hand from beneath her sweater and took her hand into his as he began to walk.

Lucky walked beside him, allowing the tears to flow down her cheeks. He was saying things she needed to hear. This affair with Cole had happened so quickly, with such force, that she'd been unprepared to love him so completely. "I...I don't want things to end for us, either. I want more, so much more."

They walked through the woods by the quietly flowing creek, the sound of trickling water mingled with autumn insects and night birds and dry, crackly leaves. The smell of fresh, cool air and earthiness encompassed them. The aroma of fried fish and lingering smoke clung to their clothes and hair.

"We'll find a way to work things out. After I've talked to the network bosses in New York, I'll come straight back to Florence. By that time we should know for sure what we want and where we're going."

She wanted to tell him that she knew now. She wanted Cole and she wanted to save Holly House. She wanted to marry him and have his children, and for them to grow old together here in her hometown. She knew the love she felt for Cole would give her the strength to overcome her fears. She couldn't lose him. She wouldn't. "We have another week before you have to leave."

"I want to spend every day and night with you. I'll help you get Holly House Antiques ready for that big pre-Christmas grand opening. And every night I'm going to sleep in your bed and make love to you and hold you in my arms." Cole stopped walking. He pulled Lucky into his arms and rubbed the side of her smooth cheek with his rough one.

She threw her arms around Cole and kissed him on the neck, her tongue tasting his skin. "Sounds wonderful to me."

"Are you cold?" he asked, pulling her closer.

"It is pretty chilly out here, but I'm getting warmer by the minute."

"Have you ever made love out in the woods at night?"

"What?" Lucky wondered if he'd lost his mind. They couldn't make love out here in the woods. Could they? The thought of it made her crazy with desire.

"We can take off your jeans and panties," he whispered. "Then I'll brace myself against one of these big trees. You wrap your legs around me and . . ."

"Oh, Cole, we couldn't." But as she said the words, Cole unzipped her jeans and tugged them and her panties to her knees.

"I want you now. Here. Like this. With a cool night breeze stimulating us, and a yellow moon casting gold shadows on your beautiful body."

"But . . . but we can't."

She was wrong. They could, and they did. Cole unzipped his jeans, and Lucky kicked her own aside as he pulled her into his arms, cradling her hips in his big hands. With one wild shove, he made them one. He took her there in the woods as an animal takes his mate, but he whispered love words only a man uniting with his equal would have uttered. It was ravishment. It was bliss. And when they reached the pinnacle of pleasure, Cole covered her mouth with his, and they swallowed each other's cries of ecstasy.

Cole leaned against the side of his Vette parked at the top of the hill. He looked out over the clearing that led to Cypress Creek. While he waited for Lucky to help her cousin Nan tuck her twin boys into bed, Cole began thinking about small-town life and families—wives and children. Lucky was the kind of woman who'd want to get married and have babies.

Suddenly he felt as if he couldn't breathe, as if some giant hand were constricting his heart and lungs. The thought of Lucky carrying his child, the image of her body swollen in pregnancy with his seed, was something he hadn't thought about. But he was thinking about it now, and it shocked him to realize how much he liked the idea. He and Kristin had agreed not to have children, at least not for a long time. He had to admit that fatherhood had been the furthest thing from his mind.

Lucky giving him a child. Yes, the more he thought about it, the more he liked the idea. But a child would mean marriage—a lifetime commitment. Was he ready for that? With Lucky it would be all or nothing. It would mean forever.

He looked up and saw Lucky stepping off the front porch of her cousin's house. She waved and smiled at him. He waved back and watched her walk toward him.

"I've always wanted to drive a Corvette," Lucky said as she approached.

"What? Drive my car? Are you crazy? Never. Not in a million years."

"Give me the keys."

"This car wouldn't start for a woman. No female has ever been behind the wheel."

Lucky grinned as she walked over and put her arms around his waist, hugging tightly. "But I'm not just any female. I'm special, remember?"

"You're not driving my Vette, honey."

Lucky slipped her hand inside his jeans pocket and curled her fingers around his key chain. "You let me drive the Vette, and I'll let you sleep in my bed tonight." She fluttered her eyelashes flirtatiously.

Cole groaned when her fingers moved around inside his pocket. "I've slept in your bed the last four nights," he said. "I wasn't aware anything had changed."

Lucky edged her fingers closer and closer to their objective. "Fishing always makes me so tired." She faked a yawn. "But driving a convertible in the night air would refresh me. Probably stimulate me all over."

Lucky's fingers hit the mark. Cole grunted, feeling himself swelling beneath her touch. "You put one dent on her, and I'll—"

"I'll treat her as if she were mine," Lucky cooed, petting him seductively. She grasped the key chain and pulled it out of his pocket. "Let's go."

Before Cole could take a deep breath and straighten his pants, Lucky was in the driver's seat.

The chilly November air ripped through Lucky's long hair, curly strands of red silk whipping the sides of her face.

"You're enjoying this, aren't you?" Cole watched Lucky. The streetlights along Florence Boulevard eliminated the darkness, allowing him to see the way her gray eyes sparkled and her creamy complexion glowed.

"Would you believe I've never driven a convertible before tonight?" Lucky pressed her foot on the accelerator and maneuvered the sports car through the heavy traffic.

"I've decided that it's worth the risk to my Vette to see you enjoying yourself so much." Cole reached out to touch the flying strands of her hair, then moved his fingers through the tumbled curls, grazing her neck as he brushed them away from her face.

Lucky turned the car off the boulevard and raced along a back street. "Could I possibly mean more to you than this car?" Lucky asked teasingly.

Cole's big hand closed over her shoulder and caressed with loving strength. "You mean more to me than anything I've ever owned." His voice was low and deep, filled with the emotions he could not hide.

Lucky turned the car onto Holly Lane, her hands trembling on the wheel. What was Cole admitting? she wondered. Not once had he told her that he loved her. Not once had he mentioned marriage. Did he need the words from her first? She wanted to tell him she loved him, had wanted to the first time they'd made love.

"Cole?"

"Hey, lady, letting you drive my Vette is only one out-ward sign of the way I feel about you." His serious tone had lightened, and a smirky grin curled the corners of his lips.

"And what are the other outward signs?" Lucky quickly reverted back to a joking mood. She drove up the long drive and parked the Vette to the side of Holly House.

"Come here, you," Cole growled playfully when Lucky parked the car and turned to look at him. His hands went around her waist, lifting her up and pulling her out of the seat. Within seconds Lucky was in Cole's lap, nestled snugly against him in the close confines of the small car. "Are you aware of any outward signs now?" He grasped her hips and pressed her into his arousal.

"You're wicked." She laughed. "What kind of man have I gotten myself involved with? He makes love in the bathtub, on the floor, in the woods against a tree. And now—"

Cole's mouth took hers, cutting off her words. The kiss was quick and hard and totally devastating. Lucky rubbed her breasts into his chest as she edged one arm around his waist, and the fingers of her other hand clutched his shoulder. When he released her mouth, both of them were breathing deeply, their mouths straining to reunite.

"Have you ever made love in a car?" he asked while his hands moved over her body with slow, tormenting provo-cation.

"No, not even as a teenager. And I'm not going to start now."

"Maybe we should drive the Vette around to the back."

Lucky tried to act shocked, pretending the idea didn't appeal to her in the least. "Cole Kendrick, I'm not going to make love in the front seat of a Corvette. Anyway, it's probably impossible."

"Oh, it's possible." He moved one big hand beneath her sweater, gently cupping the underside of her breast.

"How do you know it's possible? Have you ever made love in this car before?"

"Jealous?"

"Answer the question."

"No, honey, I've never made love in this car. I just know that with you I can make love under any circumstances."

"There's a perfectly good bed upstairs."

The sound of an approaching vehicle abruptly ended their conversation. They looked around and saw a taxi in the driveway.

"Who on earth?" Lucky watched as a very tall blonde emerged from the cab.

"Hell!" Cole held Lucky tightly, his hands so tense his grasp was almost painful.

"Who is she?" Lucky asked, stunned by the look of rage on Cole's face.

"Kristin Taylor."

"Your... your fiancée?"

"My ex-fiancée."

Lucky moved out of Cole's lap, awkwardly crawling over the console and back into the driver's seat. Her gaze moved from Cole's stricken expression to the woman in question. She had to be nearly six feet tall, but Lucky couldn't tell anything about her body because she was wrapped in a full-length white-fox coat. The coat and her long, silvery blond hair glistened like moonlight on fresh snow. When Cole opened the door and got out, Lucky didn't move. She sat immobile, her mind anesthetized by the unexpected situation.

"Cole, darling," Kristin purred as she flung her arms around Cole and kissed him passionately.

The numbness faded from Lucky's mind and heart. Pain, fierce and relentless, surged through her. She wanted to scream, to cry out, to demand her rights as Cole's lover. But the woman in his arms had once been his lover. Indeed, she'd been more. Cole had once asked Kristin Taylor to be his wife, and he hadn't even told Lucky that he loved her.

Lucky knew she couldn't keep sitting there in the car even if she were dying inside. Her brain gave orders, and her body tried to respond. *Don't cry. Move your legs. Get out of the car.* She didn't know if it took her a minute or an hour, but finally she stood beside the Corvette, her glazed eyes turning to watch the taxi drive away. She forced herself to look toward Cole and the platinum blonde who'd draped herself around him.

Nine

Serving cake and coffee to the enemy was the last thing Lucky wanted to do, but her sense of Southern hospitality overruled her desire to kick Kristin Taylor's sleek little behind out of Holly House and out of Florence. Actually what she really wanted to do was put the statuesque blonde on the fastest jet going north. The pain she'd felt earlier had faded some, replaced by a combination of hurt and anger. The whole scene seemed to be something out of a nightmare from which she couldn't awaken.

Suzy arranged small pieces of coconut cake on china plates. "You don't need to get bent out of shape over this." The young girl licked the cake knife after she'd cut the last piece. "Cole didn't invite her, and it's obvious he doesn't want her here. She's the one hanging all over him. He keeps trying to push her away."

Lucky poured fresh coffee into the cups arranged on the silver tray. She reminded herself that Cole had been surprised by his ex-fiancée's appearance, and he didn't act pleased to see her. But he hadn't asked the woman to leave and he hadn't tried too hard to disengage himself from her clutches. But what hurt most of all was that he'd introduced Lucky to the other woman as his hostess. Well, what would she have had him say—"This is my current lover"?

"Don't you dare let that bleached blond hussy get the best of you," Suzy said as she lifted the cake tray. "Why don't you put some rat poison in her coffee?"

Despite the negative emotions churning inside of her, Lucky smiled at Suzy's comment. "I hope I don't have to resort to murder to get rid of her. Besides, she's not my guest, she's Cole's. He's the one who'll have to ask her to leave."

Suzy and Lucky carried the refreshments through to the den where Uncle Pudge had escorted their guest. Kristin Taylor sat on the sofa, wedged between Pudge Prater and Cole Kendrick. Pudge was talking in his most impressive "Southern gentleman" drawl, while Cole sat rigidly, both hands in his lap. Kristin's big brown eyes focused on Uncle Pudge, a captivating smile plastered across her model-perfect face. She seemed engrossed in conversation with the elderly man, but Lucky immediately noticed the woman's slender fingers were squeezing Cole's forearm and her other hand rested on his knee.

Joel stood in a corner at the far side of the room, his blue eyes hard and watchful. Lucky took a deep breath and passed the tray around. When Cole took his cup and saucer, he looked up at Lucky, an unspoken plea for understanding in his eyes. Lucky stared back at him, silently refusing his request and issuing a demand. She wanted an explanation. She wanted reassurance. Lucky moved across the room to Joel and placed the tray on the library table flanking the back wall.

"She's not half as pretty as you," Joel whispered reassuringly.

Lucky smiled at the boy, feeling comforted by his caring even if his words held no real meaning for her.

"She may be some high-class model, but she's not half the lady you are."

"It's all right, honey."

"Lucky," Pudge called. "Come on over and join us. I was just explaining to Kristin here that Holly House isn't officially open."

Kristin's red-tipped fingers danced seductively up and down Cole's arm. "I know it would be an imposition, but couldn't you work something out where I could stay here tonight?" The blonde turned her head in Lucky's direction and smiled ever so sweetly. "After all, I've come such a long way to be with Cole. I'd even be willing to...er...to bunk in with Cole if—"

"No!" The harshly spoken response came from Cole.

"Oh, darling," Kristin said. "Even in the South, people must know that—"

"I said no, Kristin. I'll drive you to a motel. There are several very nice ones not far from here."

Lucky felt as if her heart had stopped beating, as if suddenly the world had stopped spinning.

"Well, darling, why don't you let Ms. Darnell decide. After all, this is her establishment." Kristin watched as Lucky came and sat down in the rocking chair across from the sofa.

Lucky held the delicate china cup in her hands. She was proud of her self-control. Outwardly she was calm. Not one tremble gave away the quivering within her. "I'm afraid Holly House is not open to the public, Ms. Taylor. The only room available is Co—Mr. Kendrick's. Whether you share his room or not is entirely up to him."

"Oh, my gosh, Lucky, you couldn't possibly let the two of them share a room," Suzy said in mock horror. "That would ruin Holly House's reputation before it even opens."

"I'm sorry, Miss Kristin," Uncle Pudge said after swallowing a mouthful of cake. "We are fairly open-minded down here in Dixie, but Suzy's right. My great-niece has an obligation to keep the reputation of our beloved ancestral home spotless."

"Yeah," Joel said, taking a few steps toward the center of the room. "Down here, when a man shares a room with a lady, they're either married or fixing to be."

"My goodness," Kristin said, giggling, her brown eyes sparkling with amusement. "What quaint ideas. And how very restricting they must be for you, Ms. Darnell."

"Kristin," Cole warned, forcefully removing both of her hands from his body.

"Oh, I didn't mean anything by that remark." Kristin looked from Cole's stern face to Lucky's flushed cheeks. "It's simply that Mr. Prater explained that his great-niece is a widow."

"Lucky happens to be a lady." Joel moved quickly to stand beside Lucky's chair.

"Oh, how gallant," Kristin said, forcing a smile. "You seem to have a young protector."

"My great-niece is the type of woman who brings out that trait in men. The men who love her, that is."

"Let's go, Kristin." Cole stood up, all the while never taking his eyes off Lucky. "I'll get your bags out of the foyer and drive you to a motel."

Kristin didn't budge. She watched the looks passing between Cole and Lucky. "Well, Cole, don't tell me that you've become one of Ms. Darnell's protectors."

Cole turned to Kristin, his dark eyes flashing with anger. He reached out, grabbed her by the arm and jerked her to her feet. "We're going now."

"He's so forceful, isn't he?" Kristin looked directly at Lucky when she spoke, her eyes filled with a bitterness obvious to everyone present. "But I love it when he's rough, don't you, Ms. Darnell?"

Deadly silence filled the cozy den. Cole practically dragged his ex-fiancée out of the room.

"God, what a bitch," Joel said, placing a hand on Lucky's shoulder.

They could hear the sound of Cole's rumbling voice and Kristin's syrupy cooing. Then the front door opened and closed. Lucky sat unmoving in the rocking chair, a slow, steady stream of tears cascading down her cheeks.

Suzy rushed over to Lucky and fell to her knees. She grabbed Lucky's tensely clenched hands. "Don't cry, Lucky. Please don't cry. I told you that you should have put rat poison in her coffee."

"I don't think rat poison would have worked on that one," Uncle Pudge said. "I have a feeling it would take a stake through the heart."

Lucky wanted to talk, to tell them that she loved all three of them for caring, for trying to ease her pain, but she couldn't utter a word. She realized that Kristin Taylor still wanted Cole, that she considered him her personal property. Maybe the woman actually loved Cole. If that were the case, Lucky could understand. She loved Cole herself, and she didn't want to lose him. But what would happen now? He was gone, alone with a woman who knew far more about seducing a man than Lucky ever would. Cole and Kristin had been lovers. They'd been engaged. The thought of the two of them in each other's arms, of Cole making love to the other woman, tore at Lucky's heart like buzzards feasting on a dying animal. She couldn't help but wonder what would happen when Cole got Kristin to the motel. Would he leave immediately? Would he stay? For a while? All night?

Somehow Lucky got to her feet and forced herself to walk. She wanted to be alone. She didn't want them to see her in pain. They loved her and they hurt for her.

When Joel moved to follow her, Lucky stopped, holding up a hand to warn them off. "I'm...I'm going upstairs. Alone."

When she walked out of the room, no one followed. Her legs felt as heavy as lead. She put one foot in front of the other, slowly climbing the stairs. If only she'd been able to talk to Cole before he left. She had no idea what he was thinking or feeling. She and everyone else could tell that he was upset, but Lucky needed to know more. She needed to know exactly what he was upset about and why Kristin Taylor had come to Holly House.

Lucky opened the door to her bedroom and walked across the plank floor to the window. She didn't bother to turn on a light. Soft, dim moonlight streamed through the lacy Priscilla curtains. She stood staring outside, but her eyes saw none of the nighttime beauty of stars shining through ancient tree branches or gold-kissed lawns. She saw Cole Kendrick's handsome face. He smiled. He laughed. He flirted. Lucky couldn't control the tears or the soundless sobs racking her body. Her head fell sideways onto her shoulder as she hugged herself, trying to stop the unbearable pain.

She had lost everyone she'd loved, except Uncle Pudge. She'd told herself, and she'd told Cole, that she couldn't bear to lose anything else. She'd been referring to Holly House at the time, but now she knew she'd also meant she was afraid to love Cole because she couldn't endure another loss. That's why I'm hurting, she thought. I love Cole, and whether he goes back to Kristin or not, I'm going to lose him. She'd understood from the moment they met that she was a homing pigeon and Cole was an eagle.

Lucky cried until there were no more tears, until the pain had become an ache that filled her entire body. She eased down onto the damask wing chair and curled into a ball, seeking solace and comfort from the familiar. She had come to this room, Granny's room, and sat in this chair two weeks after Granny's funeral. She had claimed the room, the chair and the heritage that was embodied in Holly House. She'd made a vow to herself, her grandmother and to every ancestor who'd lived within these walls. The house and few scant acres of land remaining would stay in the family one more generation.

Lucky heard the soft knock on her bedroom door, but before she could reply, the door opened and Uncle Pudge walked in.

"Sitting in the dark, I see." He took several cautious steps until he reached the small Tiffany lamp atop the closed antique sewing machine. He turned on the light and stood there looking at his great-niece. "Thought maybe you'd cried it all out by now and needed somebody to talk to."

She looked at him, her eyes red and puffy. "I feel drained. I don't think there are any tears left in me."

"You realize, of course, that you've blown this all out of proportion."

"Have I?" she asked, still huddled in the big chair, her feet tucked beneath her, her head resting against the chair's wing.

"That woman came of her own accord. It was plain to see that Cole didn't want her here."

"Then why did she come?"

"Hellfire, gal, she wants your man! He's going to be a big network sportscaster." Pudge stormed across the room, looking quite a bit like a bald and beardless Santa gone on a rampage.

"My man? Maybe she thinks she has a prior claim since she was his fiancée."

"Hogwash. I don't care if Cole Kendrick's been engaged or married to a dozen women, that man belongs to you."

"I wish you'd quit saying that. Just because we're lo— because we're close, doesn't mean we have any kind of claim on each other." Lucky slid her legs down the chair and let her feet touch the floor.

"You didn't have to rephrase your sentence for me, Lucky Lu. I know you and Cole are lovers. I knew from the night he came here that it was inevitable. Some things are meant to be, gal. You and Cole are one of those things."

"You're wrong. Cole and I don't have a future together. My life is here at Holly House. He has no intention of staying here permanently. He doesn't want to give up the glamour and excitement of being a celebrity."

"He'll change his mind. Just you wait and see."

"And if he doesn't?" Lucky stood up and walked to the window.

"Then you'll have to decide what you want most, Cole or Holly House." Pudge walked over to stand beside his great-niece.

She gazed out the window, this time seeing the moonlight-coated yard. "You don't understand, Uncle Pudge."

"If you're referring to the fact that the bank holds a mortgage on this place, then I do understand."

"How? Who told you?"

"Leticia and I never did have too many secrets from each other. We were always close, even as children."

"Granny told you?"

"If I hadn't been such a wastrel all my life, I'd have the money to preserve this old place. I know what's going on, why you've moved your business, why you're willing to let strangers parade in and out of here for money."

"Then you understand why I could never leave."

"That's where you're wrong." He grasped Lucky by the shoulders, turning her to face him. "This is a house, Lucky, and as much as you love it, it can't love you back. If Cole means as much to you as I think he does, then you'll go with him if he can't stay here with you."

Lucky shrugged and pulled away from her great-uncle. "None of this matters. Cole hasn't said he loves me or wants to spend the rest of his life with me. As a matter of fact, he's gone off to some motel with his ex-fiancée, or had you forgotten that little detail?"

"He'll be back."

"Before or after she seduces him?"

"Oh. So you love him, but you don't trust him."

"I...I don't know. How can I have faith in him, in what we have, if he hasn't even told me he loves me?"

"Do you need the words, gal?" The old man looked at his great-niece's sober expression and shook his head. "Yeah, I guess you do. I guess all females need the words, don't they?"

"Is that so hard to understand?"

"No, of course not. But sometimes a man thinks his woman should know how he feels by what he does, by the way he treats her. I once thought Winnie knew how I felt. I thought every time I touched her, I was telling her I loved her."

"You should have said the words, Uncle Pudge."

For endless moments neither of them spoke. Then Lucky put her arms around her great-uncle, and he held her close, stroking her hair as if she were still a child.

"Love shouldn't hurt so," Pudge said. "Dear God, it shouldn't hurt at all."

Lucky sat on the bed, her back relaxing against three feather pillows. She adjusted the tray resting across her lap and eyed the cards arranged on top of it. Her hair hung in loose, fluffy curls on her bare shoulders, caressing the gold satin of her housecoat. One by one she turned the cards over as she played a game of solitaire. When the last hidden card was revealed, she grinned, knowing victory was only seconds away.

The house was so quiet that when the grandfather clock in the downstairs hallway chimed midnight, Lucky felt as if it were striking inside her head. Each hourly signal was a reminder that Cole hadn't returned to Holly House. Where is he? she wondered. And what is he doing? After her heart-to-heart talk with Uncle Pudge, she'd taken a shower and dressed for bed, but sleep was impossible. For the past hour she'd been playing solitaire and waiting. Waiting for a man who might not come home.

Lucky grunted in disgust. She was a fool. Holly House was hardly Cole's home. He was a paying guest, and if he chose to spend the night in a motel...if he wanted to be with Kristin... Enough was enough, Lucky decided, setting the tray on the far side of the bed and hastily getting up. She had taken two steps toward the door when she heard the roar of a car's engine. She rushed to the window and peeped out. She could see Cole parking the Vette, then getting out.

Remembering that the light from her bedside lamp would reveal her presence, she moved quickly away from the window. She most certainly didn't want him to think she'd been waiting up for him. Lucky removed her housecoat and tossed it across the foot of her bed. She switched off the lamp, quickly got in bed and pulled up the covers.

Her breathing was harsh and ragged. Calm down, she told herself. Relax and pretend you're asleep.

Cole had slept in this big bed with her for the past four nights, but would he come to her tonight? she wondered. Did she want him to?

Cole knocked lightly on the outside of Lucky's closed bedroom door. He'd been disappointed when he'd come home and she hadn't been waiting for him downstairs. The house was as dark and deadly quiet as a tomb. It had taken forever to get Kristin settled in the motel with an understanding that she'd be on a flight back to New York tomorrow. They had talked, discussed past and present and finally argued. For the life of him, he couldn't understand how he ever could have thought himself in love with Kristin Taylor. What surprised him the most was that he was no longer sexually attracted to her in the least. She left him cold. He thought it odd that a woman who knew all there was to know about men didn't know the first thing about real love. He and Kristin had shared some hot sex in the past, but their times together had been nothing compared to the loving he'd shared with Lucky. Their joining was a complete union of body and soul.

When he didn't hear a response, Cole knocked again lightly. He turned the brass doorknob and eased the door open slightly. The room was dark except for the shimmering moonlight.

"Lucky," he called out softly.

There was no reply. Surely she wasn't asleep. He knew she'd been shocked and hurt by Kristin's unexpected appearance. He'd thought she'd be waiting up with a hundred questions.

"Lucky, honey?" He opened the door, stepped into the bedroom and closed the door behind him.

The moonlight gave enough illumination that he could see the shape of the furniture. He walked to the bed and looked down. Lucky was covered up to her neck. Her eyes were closed, and she was breathing slowly. She's not asleep, he thought. She's pretending. Well, that meant she was very angry.

"Lucky, I know you're awake."

She didn't move or speak.

Cole reached out and flipped on the bedside lamp. "I know you're probably wondering why Kristin came here and why it took me so long to get away from her." Cole sat down on the bed.

She moved away from him. "Hmph . . ."

"I didn't ask her to come here. I didn't want to see her."

Lucky turned her back on Cole, the covers slipping slightly to reveal the gold satin of her nightgown.

Cole placed his hand on her shoulder and felt her stiffen. "She's flying back to New York tomorrow. She made a mistake coming here, and now she realizes it."

"I guess it's difficult to juggle two lovers at the same time," Lucky said, jerking free of his hold to sit upright in the bed. When she did, the tray and playing cards fell to the floor with a loud bump.

"Kristin and I haven't been lovers since before my accident." Cole looked at Lucky, and cold fear enveloped him. He realized that she was more than hurt and angry. She was livid. Her pale cheeks were flushed pink, and her eyes were swollen from crying. He wanted to hold her, kiss her and love her. He wanted to make her understand that she was the only woman in the world for him.

"Well, you had plenty of time tonight to remedy that, didn't you?"

"I didn't make love to Kristin tonight!" Cole raised his voice, anger vibrating the tone.

"Are you saying she didn't try to seduce you?" Lucky glared at him, her gray eyes silver flames.

"I...what the hell difference does that make? I told you we didn't make love."

"Then she did try to seduce you, didn't she?"

"Hell. Okay, yes. She made the offer, but—"

"Then I don't understand why you're not still with her."

"Dammit, Lucky, I don't want Kristin. She's a part of my past."

"Oh, but if you take that network job, she could be a part of your future. She'd like that kind of life, wouldn't she? She'd still be marrying a celebrity."

"I'm not marrying Kristin whether I take the network offer or not."

"Did you tell her that?"

"What?"

"Did you tell her that you don't ever intend to marry her?"

"Yes. I told her that over a year ago." Cole reached out and took Lucky by the shoulders. God, she felt so warm and soft, so totally woman.

"Obviously she doesn't believe you. Why is that, I wonder?" Lucky twisted, trying to free herself from his hold.

He held her tightly. "Kristin's just coming out of an affair with one of my old teammates. She was hoping to rekindle our flame." Cole pulled Lucky into his arms.

Although she held her body rigid against him, she didn't try to pull away. "If you, if you want her..."

"I want you, Lucille Leticia Llewellyn Darnell." He felt her body soften into his. He could feel the rise and fall of her breasts against him.

"Why did you stay so long? All I could think of was the two of you making love." Lucky buried her face in his chest, her arms going about his waist.

"Oh, God, honey, I'm sorry. I wanted to make sure Kristin understood how things stand between us. I stayed until she agreed to leave tomorrow."

"She still loves you, doesn't she?" Lucky held him close, her fingers biting into his back through his sweater.

"She still wants me. There's a difference. I know now that what I shared with Kristin wasn't love." Cole planted a series of light kisses in Lucky's hair, moving down to her forehead when she turned her face up to him.

"I . . . I want you to leave," Lucky mumbled the words, looking directly into his eyes, her arms still holding him.

"What?" He knew he must have misunderstood what she'd said.

Lucky eased her body from his, releasing her hold on him. "I'm tired. I'm still angry, still hurting from... I can't handle this. Not now."

"Are you asking me to leave your bedroom or leave Holly House?" He couldn't bear the thought that she was asking him to do either. He wanted nothing more than to make love to her tonight and every night until he had to go to New York.

"Both." When he tried to keep her from moving away from him, she brushed his hands aside. "You and I have separate futures. We need to concentrate on making decisions that will affect the rest of our lives."

"I don't have to be in New York for another few days." He knew he was begging, but he didn't care. He didn't want Lucky to end their relationship. Not now. Not yet.

"There's no point in prolonging the inevitable," she said, chewing on the inside of her mouth, trying not to let fresh tears fall.

"There has to be a way for us, honey. I don't want what we've found to end like this."

"Go to New York. Talk to the networks. Make a final decision." Her hand trembled when she reached out to touch his face. "I know where my life is going. It's all mapped out. I'm going to keep Holly House no matter what I have to do. If my shop and the holiday tours don't bring in enough for the January payment, I'm going to Atlantic City."

"I could loan you the money you need."

"No, that isn't an option for me. Like I said, my life is planned. You're the one who needs to get his life in order. When you do, we'll both know where we stand."

His flesh burned beneath her gentle touch. He wanted to pull her back into his arms and never let her go. But he understood how she felt. He'd known all along that Lucky wasn't a woman for brief affairs. She'd told him so herself. She was a forever-after kind of woman. Could he offer her what she needed and deserved? "I'll drive back to Memphis tomorrow and fly to New York in a few days."

"You'll call me?" she asked, tiny drops of moisture forming in the corners of her eyes.

"I'll call." He savored the feel of her fingers on his face, knowing how much he would miss this woman's caresses. "When everything is settled, I'll come back. Whatever we decide about our futures, it should be face-to-face...together."

"Yes, you're right." She dropped her hand from his face. "Please go to your room. I...I can't..."

"Let me stay. I promise we won't make love unless...I won't do anything you don't want me to. I promise."

"I...I don't know. Cole, I..." Lucky tried to stop the tears the moment she felt them building in her eyes. Dear God, she thought there weren't any left within her.

He pulled her into his arms and held her while she cried. The sound tore at his insides, gutting him, destroying him by degrees. "Oh, honey, don't. Joel was right from the very beginning. I'm not good enough for you. I've hurt you, and that was the last thing on earth I wanted."

"Cole... Cole..." She sobbed his name over and over again.

He lay back against the pillows, taking her with him, her warm body resting in the curve of his. She·lay in his arms and cried while he stroked and petted her, all the while whispering tender words of caring. The two of them lay entwined until sleep overcame Lucky after she'd emptied her soul of its pain.

Cole held her, watching her in slumber, knowing and yet afraid to admit how much she meant to him. They hadn't shared the words. They hadn't made a commitment. His future was in sportscasting, moving around the country. Her future was Holly House. How could he ask her to give up something that meant everything to her?

The thought of a life without Lucky seemed meaningless. Staying on the road, traveling from city to city, had lost its appeal during the weeks he'd spent in Florence. There was a great deal to be said for quiet, peaceful living in a small Southern town. For the past few weeks he'd actually been considering checking into the job Uncle Pudge had told him about—the coaching position open at the University of North Alabama. When Pudge had first mentioned it, Cole had dismissed the idea. But the more he thought about it, the more appealing it became.

There wasn't big money in college coaching at a small school, and there'd be no fame and very little glory. But he didn't need the money, and it surprised him to realize he no longer craved the fame and glory.

He'd have to go to New York. He'd have to talk to the networks. A few weeks away from Lucky might be good for them both. He needed to do some serious thinking about his future, and she had to save her beloved Holly House.

The thought of her gambling her savings in Atlantic City on the chance she'd win enough to pay the January mortgage made him want to strangle her. Why the hell couldn't she just take the money from him? If she weren't so stubborn, so all-fired determined to do things on her own . . .

An hour later Cole finally slept, a restless, fitful sleep full of dreams of a lonely life without Lucky.

A little before dawn Lucky awoke with the feel of Cole's big body pressing against her and his hot breath on her neck.

"Cole?" She called his name in drowsy confusion.

"I want you," he whispered as he raised his head and looked down at her.

"Oh." Her eyes flew open completely.

"Will you let me make love to you before I go?" His lips hovered above hers, his dark eyes pleading.

Lucky threw her arms around his neck and pulled him down to her. His lips captured hers with a wildness that set her afire. When Cole's hands moved beneath her nightgown, slowly edging up the inside of her thigh, Lucky broke the kiss and eased her lips away from his. He squeezed her thigh, his thumb pressing against the soft folds of her femininity. She opened herself to the gentle probing of his fingers, her own hands tugging on his sweater. He removed his sweater and shirt, leaving his hairy chest bare for Lucky's eager touch. Her fingers slid through the thick mass of curls adorning his body.

"Oh, God, woman, you're in my heart, in my mind day and night. I want to make love to you again and again."

"I can't get enough of you, either," she admitted, her tongue flicking across his pebble-hard nipple.

Cole pushed her gown up to her waist and lowered a strap to reveal the pouting crest of one breast. He unzipped his jeans and pulled them off along with his briefs. "I want to be inside you—now!"

Lucky took the full length of his passion as he thrust into her waiting warmth. "Yes, yes," she moaned as he moved in and out of her with hard, driving plunges.

"You're mine," he told her just before he slowed his frantic stabs and lowered his lips to her breast.

"Cole!" she cried out when he took her nipple into his mouth, sending shivers of desire through her feverish body.

He sucked greedily, then switched breasts to give equal tribute. Lucky's hips moved in perfect rhythm with him. Male and female, they become one. One heart, one mind, one soul. He raised his head and looked down at her face as he moved within her. "Tell me how much you want me. Tell me while I'm deep inside you," he groaned, then kissed her, thrusting his tongue into her mouth as he thrust his manhood into her receptive body.

"I want you . . . want you so . . ."

The tempo of their lovemaking steadily increased as Cole murmured incoherent words and phrases of heated passion until she, and then he, reached the peak. Lucky moaned, her body trembling with the force of her release. The pleasure of her completion was so great that her body jerked with continuing spasms of ecstasy as Cole poured his seed into her. His body trembled as he cried out her name and collapsed into the softness of her sweat-damp body. After a few minutes they both began to recover from the death of passion. Cole slid off her and snuggled at her side, holding her in his arms.

Lucky curled against him, replete, sleep already overtaking her as she whispered into the predawn darkness, "I want you." Silently she added, "I want you forever, my love."

Lucky woke with a start. The sound of a car engine aroused her from a sound sleep. Bright morning sunshine poured in the windows. She turned and saw that the other side of her bed was empty. She jumped out of bed and raced to the window. Cole was turning his Vette around in the driveway. Oh, God, he's leaving, she thought. Her lips were silent as her heart protested his departure. Lucky grabbed her delicate silk gown from the floor and slipped into it. She ran out of the bedroom and down the stairs. She flung open the door just in time to see the Corvette nearing the end of the driveway. She ran onto the veranda and called out Cole's name. The car disappeared up the long, curving drive.

The brisk November air chilled Lucky to the bone as the morning breeze swirled around her nearly naked body. Her gold nightgown clung to her legs as the wind whipped her long hair about her face. She stood, silent and alone, knowing that her life would never be the same again. Cole was gone.

Ten

$\underline{}$

Lucky looked at the column of figures, hoping that by some miracle the totals would change. But they didn't. During the past few weeks while she endured the Thanksgiving and Christmas holidays without Cole, trying to earn enough money for the January mortgage payment on Holly House had kept her sane. But now, she knew she had failed. Even with the successful reopening of her antique shop and the numerous holiday tours, the totals printed in black and white didn't lie. She was still several thousand dollars short of the sum needed to save Holly House.

Lucky crumpled the paper in her hand and tossed it into the wastebasket by her desk. Every day for weeks, she had checked and double-checked the figures. Several days ago she came to the conclusion that she'd have to activate her backup plan. She was booked on tomorrow's flight to Atlantic City via Atlanta.

Miss Winnie had offered her a loan and so had Rich, but she couldn't accept their money any more than she'd been able to accept Cole's. It was her responsibility to save Holly House, and she intended to use her *talent* to do just that. She'd fly to Atlantic City, use her savings to play twenty-one, win just enough to make the mortgage payment and cover her expenses, stay the night and fly home the next day. She had it all figured out, down to the last detail. Except for one thing. How was she going to tell Cole her decision and make him understand?

During the first two weeks after Cole had left, he'd called her almost every day. Recently the phone calls stopped, and Lucky had begun to worry, wondering if he'd decided a long-distance affair wouldn't be worth the effort. All her old fears and uncertainties had surfaced. She was afraid she'd lose Cole.

Then he'd called yesterday, Christmas Day, and told her he was with his sister in Memphis and the two of them were driving down to Florence so Becky and Lucky could meet. Lucky expected their arrival at any moment. Part of her couldn't wait to see Cole again, to hold him in her arms, to tell him how much she loved and needed him. But a part of her didn't want to hear any news about his sportscasting job, about his future plans. And she certainly dreaded telling him about her trip. She knew he'd never understand that going to Atlantic City really wouldn't be much of a gamble. The odds had always been in Lucky Darnell's favor whenever her fingers touched the cards.

She was thankful she'd been so busy during the weeks since Cole left that only at night, alone in her bed, had she found time to weep for the loneliness in her soul. During the precious days they'd shared, Cole had become the center of her universe, the very heartbeat of her existence. What would she do if she lost him? Could she live through one more loss and survive?

Not only did her heart and soul yearn for Cole Kendrick, but her body ached with the need to be joined with his. She had already decided that if Cole was willing to continue with a part-time affair, she would agree. She couldn't imagine her life without him. She was willing to accept whatever he had to offer. After all, what else could a woman so desperately in love do?

"I see Cole's Vette coming up the drive," Suzy said as she ran into the den, interrupting Lucky's thoughts. "Come on, Lucky. Hurry. You'll want to be on the porch waiting for him."

Lucky hesitated briefly, so many doubts and fears swirling through her brain. Suzy tugged on Lucky's arm, urging her to move.

"All right. All right. I'm coming." Lucky stood up, Suzy's hand still on her arm, and let the girl lead her out into the hall.

"Uncle Pudge and Joel are already outside. Oh, Lucky, aren't you excited? Cole's come home, and he's brought his sister to meet you. You know what that means, don't you?"

"No, what does that mean?" Lucky stopped when Suzy swung open the front door.

"Well, she's all the family he's got, so before he pops the question, he wants you two to meet." Suzy pulled Lucky through the door and out onto the veranda.

Lucky watched as Cole stopped the Vette in the driveway at the front of the house. He got out and waved, smiling up at Lucky. Her heart lodged in her throat. He looked so unbelievably wonderful in a pair of dark slacks and a tweed sport coat. Desire churned in Lucky's bloodstream. She wanted nothing more than to run down the steps and throw herself into his arms. Crazy thoughts of making wild love with him on the hood of the Vette dashed through her mind, and she blushed at her own torrid imagination.

Cole walked around the car and opened the passenger door. A tall, strikingly beautiful brunette stepped out. The resemblance between Cole and his younger sister stunned Lucky. Rebecca Kendrick could have been Cole's twin. Her style, however, was one of cool sophistication. She wore black leather boots and a classically tailored black suit with a colorful woolen shawl draped over one shoulder.

Rebecca's dark eyes scanned the group of people standing on the veranda. Her gaze caught Lucky's, and when Lucky smiled at her, Rebecca smiled back.

Cole took his sister's arm and started walking toward the porch. Lucky couldn't stop herself from moving down the steps, and when she reached the yard, her footsteps picked up speed. Cole released his sister's arm and moved hurriedly toward Lucky. He reached out and grabbed her, pulling her into his arms, hugging her fiercely as her arms circled his neck. They looked at each other for a split second, weeks of loneliness and deprivation shared in that one exchange.

"God, how I've missed you, woman!" Cole growled. Then his mouth took hers with the greediness of a starving man.

Lucky clung to him, eagerly opening her mouth, her tongue making love to his while the world faded far away. Her only coherent thought was that Cole had come home and he was in her arms where he belonged.

Finally Cole broke the kiss, his lips only inches above hers. "Missed me, too, huh?"

Lucky opened her eyes and looked up at him. He grinned. She laughed. "My bed's been awfully empty," she whispered.

"Well, now that you two have gotten that out of the way, how about introducing us to this pretty gal," Uncle Pudge said, walking up and extending his hand to Rebecca. "I'm Jefferson Davis Prater, but my friends call me Pudge. You can call me Uncle Pudge."

Rebecca shook the old man's hand with enthusiasm. "Hello, Uncle Pudge. It's so nice to meet you. Cole's told me all about you."

"Not the bad things, too, boy?" Pudge took Rebecca's arm and led her up the steps onto the veranda. He turned around and shook his head. He grunted when he looked at Lucky and Cole still wrapped in each other's arms. "You two coming in, or you going to stand out there and freeze to death?"

"I hope you understand why we didn't make it down yesterday for Christmas," Rebecca said, sitting in the rocking chair by the fireplace in Lucky's den. "Cole knew how important it was for me to help at the shelter. I was already obligated, and he gallantly volunteered to go and help out even though he wanted to be with you."

Lucky put another log on the fire and replaced the glass screen. "I can understand why it was important to you. Cole told me that you do a great deal of volunteer work at shelters for abused women and children."

"Yes." Rebecca gazed into the flickering fire. "I know that Cole told you about our father."

"Some. But I'm sure there are things he may never be able to share with anyone, not even me, as much I care for him."

"Oh, Lucky, you don't how glad I am that he's found someone like you. Once, his life was overrun with Kristin Taylors. And after the accident, I worried about his attitude toward everything. I was afraid he'd never get his life on the right track. You've worked wonders on my brother. I've never seen him so happy.''

"That's because I've never known a woman like Lucky,'' Cole said, walking into the room, Pudge directly behind him.

Lucky felt the heat flushing her face while her heart beat wildly, savoring Cole's words.

Cole sat down on the couch beside Lucky and pulled her into his arms.

"You two are disgusting,'' Pudge said teasingly. "We have two innocent teenagers out in the kitchen fixing lunch for us, and here y'all are carrying on in broad daylight.''

Cole kissed Lucky passionately, and Rebecca laughed when Pudge winked at her.

Snuggling against Cole, Lucky looked over at Rebecca. "I'm so glad you came with Cole. I...I hope you can stay long enough for us to get to know each other.'' Lucky wanted to ask Cole how long he would be staying, but she lacked the courage. Perhaps his sister could furnish the answer.

"I'm afraid I've got to go back to Memphis tomorrow, but I promise I'll come back very soon for a longer stay. I have appointments scheduled every day the rest of the week.''

"I've told her she works too hard, but how do you get a lady shrink to take time off? She's always got an answer for everything.'' Cole knew his sister's job was her whole world, and that without it, she would be lost. She had no husband, no children and very little social life. Their old man had really done a number on her, all right. If only Becky could find someone special the way he had.

During the weeks he'd been apart from Lucky, he'd come to realize exactly how much he'd changed since his accident, and especially since coming to Holly House. It shocked him to think that he was actually considering making his relationship with Lucky permanent. They'd have a lot of problems to work through, and each of them would have to give a little, compromise some. But he was willing to try, if Lucky was. Already he'd taken steps to ensure their future—to make certain they'd never have to be apart. A couple of months ago he never would have considered giving up his chance at being a celebrity again. But Lucky had made him realize he wanted more from life.

"I'm not a shrink," Rebecca said. "I'm a child psychologist."

"I stand corrected," her brother said.

Cole hoped Becky and Lucky would hit it off in a big way, and so far they seemed to be doing just that. He wanted Lucky's enthusiasm and exuberance for life and love to show his sister what a woman's life could be like without any leftover emotional baggage from a battered childhood. It seemed to him that Becky could help other people deal with the tragedies of abuse, but even with all her training, she'd never been able to put the past behind her completely. At least not enough to trust any man with her heart.

"You're not leaving tomorrow, are you, boy?" Pudge asked.

"Nope. The length of my stay will depend on a certain fiery redhead we both know." Cole nuzzled the side of Lucky's neck.

Oh, Lord, what does he mean by that? Lucky wondered. He must know that she wanted him to stay forever. "I . . . I want you to stay here for as long as you can."

Cole leaned over and kissed her on the ear, then whispered, "After lunch, you and I are going upstairs."

Shivers of excitement raced up Lucky's spine at the thought of being alone with Cole. She turned her head, lowered her voice to a hush and said, "Yes."

"And we're not coming down till morning."

"Not till morning." A cold and clutching fear shook Lucky. Cole had come back to her, but for how long? She wanted to hold him, bind him to her and never let him go. But she knew the tighter you held a man like Cole Kendrick, the harder he'd fight to loosen the ties. She was gambling her heart once again, and she had no idea whether she would win or lose.

"Lunch is ready," Joel Haney announced from the doorway. "Suzy's fixed everything up real fancy in the dining room. In your honor, Ms. Kendrick."

"How sweet of her," Rebecca said. "But y'all didn't have to go to any extra trouble for me. I'm practically family." She looked at her brother and the woman in his arms and smiled.

Lucky lay naked and sated in Cole's loving arms. Shadows of early evening filled the corners of her bedroom as the last rays of winter sunshine spread a tawny glow across the wooden floor. If six months ago anyone had told Lucky that she would have meekly followed a man up to her bedroom in the middle of the day and spent hours making hot, wild love, she would have thought them crazy. But that's exactly what she'd done. And she had left four people downstairs who knew precisely why she'd come upstairs. The whole thing was Cole's fault. He wasn't just any man. He was special. She loved him with a passion she'd never known existed before he came into her life.

Lucky still didn't know where their relationship was headed, if anywhere. There had been little time for talk, both of them far too eager to make love to waste time on mere words. They said with their bodies what words could never say. And yet only words could erase her fears and doubts. Only words could tell her what she wanted to know and was afraid to find out. Only words could bind them together or set them both free to go their separate ways.

"You can't imagine how much I've missed you," Cole murmured, one hand covering her breast beneath the quilts, and the other stroking her shoulder.

"Yes, I can. I've missed you just as much."

"I don't want us to ever again be apart that long." He teased her nipple and listened to the sound of her sensual groan.

"But if you're traveling all over the country on your new job—"

He silenced her with a kiss, then eased away from her and smiled. "There is no reason why we can't be together every day while I'm working."

Surely he wasn't expecting her to travel with him, to give up her commitments here at Holly House? He knew she couldn't do that. "Cole, I can't leave here. Not yet."

"Not yet?"

"I . . . I have to pay off the loan first." *What am I saying?* she wondered. *Did I really mean that? Yes,* she knew she did. If Cole was willing to wait another year until she had the mortgage paid off, she'd leave Holly House in Uncle Pudge's care until they could find a buyer who loved the old place and would maintain it as a family home. Her great-uncle had been right. No matter how much she loved Holly House, it couldn't love her back. And, by God, she wasn't going to lose a man who could.

"Are you saying you'd leave Holly House and travel with me once you pay off the mortgage on this place?" Cole moved away from her and sat up in the bed, the sheet and quilts slipping low on his hips.

"Yes, that's exactly what I'm saying." Lucky looked up at him, her eyes filled with shiny tears. "I don't want to lose you."

Cole stared at her as if he couldn't believe his own ears. "You'd actually give up Holly House, leave behind everything and everyone? You'd be willing to change your whole life...for me?''

"Yes."

Cole laughed, the sound one of a man rejoicing in the knowledge that he came first in his woman's life. He reached down and pulled her up into his arms, hugging her to him, her bare breasts crushed against his hairy chest. "You're one hell of a woman, Lucky Darnell."

Cole had every right to know that she planned to fly to Atlantic City tomorrow. But she didn't want to ruin this moment, this precious moment that would never come again. She decided that morning would be soon enough to tell him. "Let's talk in the morning. Right now I have other plans." She ran her fingers up and down his chest, twining them around his chest hairs.

"A woman after my own heart." Cole ran one finger down her throat and between her breasts. Tomorrow he'd give her the money to pay off the mortgage on Holly House, and she'd be free of her past, free to be with him.

"After your heart and after that fantastic body of yours, too." She let her fingers trail downward past his stomach, stopping at his navel. Her fingertip moved a fraction of an inch and touched him.

He sucked in his breath. "You do know what you're asking for, don't you, honey?" Cole asked playfully.

"Oh, yes."

"Then I can assure you that you're going to get it."

"Promises, promises," she teased as she took his maleness in her hand, encompassing its quickly growing hardness.

With one deft move, Cole flipped Lucky onto her back and mounted her, his hairy knee parting her legs as his mouth descended to her breast. "Let's set the world on fire."

"Oh, we will. We will." Lucky took him in her hand again and guided him into her body. She welcomed him with all the love and passion in her heart, uncertain of tomorrow and deathly afraid of losing Cole.

"What the hell do you mean you're flying to Atlantic City today?" Cole demanded, his black eyes glowing like polished onyx.

"My flight leaves for Atlanta in two hours. I've got to finish packing, or I'll miss the plane."

"You damn well can miss it. You aren't going!"

"What?"

"You heard me. I forbid you to go."

"You what?"

Cole knew he'd said the wrong thing and wished he could rephrase his last remark. "There's no need for you to go to Atlantic City and risk losing your savings."

"If you could just be reasonable about his," Lucky said, still standing beside her open suitcase on the bed. "I'll be back tomorrow with enough money to take care of the January payment."

Cole glared at her, his shoulders resting against the closed door. "Why risk losing your money when you don't have to? Let me take care of this for you."

"The chances that I'll lose are practically nonexistent. Besides, Holly House isn't your responsibility."

He shoved his hands in his jeans pockets, leaned his head back against the door and clenched his teeth. "Take the damn money from me." What's the matter with her? he wondered. I've got the money. She needs it. She's mine, and a man takes care of his own.

Lucky took several tentative steps toward Cole. "I can't." Perhaps, once the deed was done, she could make him see reason. She was going to Atlantic City today, and only an act of God would stop her. Even if nobody understood her reasoning, she knew if she didn't take responsibility for Holly House and the promise she'd made Granny, she would never be free from the past.

Lucky walked over and stopped directly in front of Cole. He eased away from the door and ran his fingertips across her cheek.

"Why can't you just let me give you the money?" he asked. "It would be so simple. I wouldn't even miss it."

"No."

"I thought you were willing to give up everything for me. Were you lying when you told me that?"

"No, I wasn't lying. I will give up everything, just as soon as I secure Holly House's future. I have to keep my promise to Granny."

"Take my goddamn money!"

"I can't."

"Why not? It's only money. Does your pride mean more to you than I do?"

"I could ask you the same question."

"Hell! I wish I could understand. I wish... Why do you have to be so stubborn?"

I will not cry, she told herself. She couldn't allow her feelings for Cole to weaken her resolve. She knew what she had to do. Even if it meant losing Cole, she had an obligation to the past that superseded their relationship. "Will you wait here... until I come back?" Please, please, she prayed silently, let him say yes.

"Don't go, Lucky." His lips nuzzled her neck while his fingers ran through the silken mass of her auburn curls. He clutched a handful of her hair so tightly that she cried out in pain. "Don't do this to us."

He loosened his hurtful grasp on her hair as he guided her head upward toward his. His mouth covered hers swiftly, harshly, as the kiss pleaded and demanded and warned. Lucky returned the kiss with equal passion, her mouth begging for his understanding, promising bliss and asserting independence.

The sound of knocking ended the kiss.

"If we're going to get to the airport before the plane takes off without you, we'd better get going," Uncle Pudge said through the closed door.

"I'll be down in a minute," Lucky said. "I'm almost through packing."

She pulled out of Cole's arms and walked across the room. Hurriedly she finished packing and closed the suitcase. When she turned around, Cole stood in the open doorway looking at her as if he were debating whether or not to lock her in her bedroom.

"There's nothing I can say or do that will change your mind, is there?" he asked.

She clutched the suitcase in her hand, squared her shoulders and walked toward the door. "No."

"I'll probably drive Becky to Memphis today. She'd planned to rent a car and drive back alone, but... Well, since you're leaving, there's no need for me to stay, is there?"

With head held high, she walked past him and out the door into the hallway. She wanted to cry and plead, to beg him to stay. She wanted a life with him more than anything, but... When this was over, she'd go to him in Memphis or even in New York. She'd be damned if she'd let his single-minded stupidity end their relationship.

"You go ahead and drive Becky home to Memphis," Lucky said, her back to him. "If you can't stay at Holly House and wait for me, then I'll come to Memphis."

"You're assuming I'll be in Memphis."

"Are you flying back to New York?"

"I didn't say that."

She set the suitcase on the floor and turned to him. "Where will you be tomorrow?" she asked, her gray eyes clear and bright, her face devoid of emotion.

"Do you really care?"

"Dammit, Cole, you're acting like a little boy."

She could tell that statement stung. The frown creasing his brow and the heated glare aimed directly at her told Lucky he was fighting to control his temper.

"Go to Atlantic City. Lose your savings. Lose Holly House, but don't think I'm going to be waiting around for a woman who puts me second in her life."

He walked past her and down the stairs. Lucky didn't move for several minutes. She let his words soak in as the pain began to build inside her. Well, what had she expected? After all these years, she should know that Lucille Leticia Llewellyn Darnell could never keep the people she loved. Somehow, someway, she always lost. She'd sworn she wouldn't lose Cole, but the very past that she was trying to put to rest was taking him away from her.

Finally she knew the answer to a question she'd been asked countless times. "If you're lucky at cards, are you unlucky in love?" She'd loved only two men in her thirty years. One had died, and the other...

She picked up her suitcase and walked downstairs to where Uncle Pudge stood waiting.

Eleven

"Here, drink this. It's strong and hot," Rebecca Kendrick told her brother as she handed him the steaming mug of coffee. "And don't think you're leaving my apartment until we talk it all out. I've already called Keela and told her to cancel my next two appointments."

"You didn't have to do that, Becky." Cole sat on the edge of the chair, balancing the mug on his knee.

"Yes, I did." Rebecca pulled up another chrome kitchen chair and sat down directly in front of her brother. "I couldn't get you to say more than a dozen words on the drive from Florence. As soon as Uncle Pudge and Lucky left for the airport, you rushed out the door like a madman."

"There wasn't any reason to stick around." Cole took a sip of coffee, then set the mug on the chrome-and-glass table. During the three-hour drive to Memphis, Cole began regretting the stand he'd taken with Lucky. When he'd gone to Holly House yesterday, he'd intended to tell her that he wanted a future with her. But what had he done? He'd acted like some damn macho idiot.

Rebecca unbuttoned her suit coat, removed it and hung it on the back of her chair. "You're upset because she wouldn't take the money from you to pay off Holly House's mortgage. Right?"

"She thinks, because the money from the loan paid off her dead husband's bills, it's her sole responsibility to earn the money to meet the mortgage payments. Can you figure it? What the hell difference does it make where the money comes from?"

"I understand how she feels," Rebecca said, putting a spoonful of sugar in her coffee. "I'd feel the same way if I were in her shoes."

Cole looked at his sister as if she'd suddenly turned into the wicked witch of the West. "You would?"

"Yes, I would." Rebecca poured a liberal amount of cream into her coffee.

"Figures."

"Uncle Pudge told me how Lucky got her nickname. Actually we had a nice long talk about the two of you." Rebecca stood up and walked over to the refrigerator. "Would you like some brunch? How about an omelet?"

"I'm not hungry. What did you and Uncle Pudge talk about?"

"Mostly about how glad we are that you and Lucky found each other. We agreed that it's rare for two people to find the kind of love and passion you two obviously share." She took a carton of eggs out and set it on the counter.

"I never said anything about being in love." Cole clutched the coffee mug in his big hands and gazed down into the black liquid.

"You may be my dearly loved brother, Cole Kendrick, but you're an awfully stupid man if you can't even admit to yourself that you're head-over-heels in love with Lucky."

"She's never said anything about love."

Rebecca rolled her eyes heavenward and groaned. "I'll bet you didn't even tell her about your new job, did you?"

"I was going to tell her, but she surprised me by saying she'd leave Holly House and Florence to follow me all over the country if I'd give her a year to pay off the mortgage."

"Sounds like a lady who has her priorities straight. It doesn't sound like a woman putting her man second. It sounds like a mature, responsible adult taking charge of her own life."

"I wish you wouldn't talk like that. You sound so damn smart."

"I am smart. I've got a Ph.D. to prove it." Rebecca beat the eggs into a frothy concoction and poured them into a buttered omelet pan.

"Why don't you get yourself a man and stay out of my love life? It's time you quit freezing out every man who comes along."

"I've never met anyone special," Rebecca said, carefully folding the omelet. "But if I ever love someone the way you love Lucky, I'll never let him go."

"You think I should drive back to Holly House and be waiting for her when she comes home tomorrow?"

She turned the omelet out on a plate and set the plate in front of her brother. She handed him a fork. "Here, you eat while I make a phone call."

"Who're you calling?"

Rebecca picked up the receiver from the wall phone, flipped through the pages of the telephone directory and dialed a number. "Yes, I'd like to make reservations for your first available flight to Atlantic City. Good. Yes, thank you. The name is Cole Kendrick.''

Cole dropped the fork. It made a clinking sound as it hit the side of the plate. He listened, openmouthed with astonishment.

His sister hung up the phone and turned to him. "Finish eating. Then take a shower and change clothes.''

"Just why the hell did you do that? I'd rather drive back to Florence and wait for her at Holly House.''

"Oh, no, you're not. You're going to Atlantic City. Lucky needs you. Take my word for it. I'm a woman and a psychologist. I know these things.''

"Rebecca Jane Kendrick, you've turned into a damn smart aleck.''

Laughing, Rebecca leaned over and hugged her brother.

Lucky pulled the black panty hose up around her waist, tossed on her black half-slip and reached for the glass of water sitting on the dressing table. She took several sips and put the glass down. She looked in the mirror, quickly double-checking her makeup and running her fingers through her hair. I need to put this mess up, she thought.

She walked across the stylish hotel room, stopped at the foot of the bed and picked up her black velvet dress. She slipped it on over her head and adeptly zipped up the back. She checked her watch, and then glanced at the clock on the nightstand. The timepieces were within two minutes of each other. She sat down on the edge of the bed and lowered her head, covering her face with both hands.

In a few hours this will all be over, she told herself. In the morning, I'll go home. But would Cole still be at Holly House? Somehow she doubted it. He'd probably be on a plane headed for New York by this time tomorrow.

Lucky knew she shouldn't be nervous about gambling, but she was. She'd played and won every type of card game under the sun. This shouldn't be all that different just because it was in some fancy casino with glittering lights and sophisticated people. She knew what she had to do. She'd simply buy her chips, place her bets and haul in her winnings. She felt so alone and so much like a small-town girl lost in the big city. She didn't like big cities and huge crowds of strangers. She liked small, friendly towns where most people were at least nodding acquaintances.

She jumped up, straightened her dress and walked over to the dressing table. She took several bobby pins out of her overnight case, twisted her long hair into a Gibson-girl knot and secured it with the pins. There, that's better, she thought. The small diamond-and-pearl earrings were more noticeable with her hair up.

Five minutes later she stepped out of the elevator and moved quickly through the din of assorted people, ranging from the sleek and elegant to the average tourist to a variety of seedy characters. Lucky wasn't a drinker, but she was tempted to go into the nearby lounge for some liquid courage. No, she decided, the best thing was to go straight into the casino and get started.

Aisles of slot machines and countless gaming tables filled her line of vision as she entered the enormous casino. She could feel her palms dampening and her heartbeat accelerating. As she passed a crowded craps table, she could smell the strong odor of whiskey. She supposed, if she weren't here on a mission, she could enjoy the glitz and glamour of it all. But even as bright and glittery as it was, it was a phony world, a playground for anyone wanting temporary excitement.

It was after ten, and the casino was filled with eager spenders, thrill seekers and gamblers. Lucky noticed the security people with their walkie-talkies, and heard bells ringing and coins clanging, but didn't look around to see who had just won at a nearby slot machine.

She stopped at a blackjack table. She wanted to watch for a while, soak in the atmosphere and get a feel for the place. The dealer, an attractive man in his late forties, dealt the cards to the four players.

Lucky moved in a bit closer and observed several more hands before she took a hundred dollars from her black sequin bag and bought chips from the dealer. When the cards were dealt, Lucky looked at her hand and smiled. An ace and the queen of hearts—a natural. She won the first deal without even trying. Well, I didn't get the nickname Lucky for nothing, she thought.

Lucky won the second hand with two tens. The players tossed their cards to the dealer. She bet again, and won when the dealer went over. On the fourth hand she let it stand with seventeen and beat the dealer, who had sixteen. Quickly she calculated how much she'd won in the short time she'd been playing. She prayed silently that her luck would hold out just a little longer.

Deciding to play it safe, she started betting only a portion of her chips on each play, which proved a wise move when she lost the fifth hand. Everything seemed to be moving so fast, too fast for a small-town girl used to playing blackjack for fun instead of profit. She didn't play the next few hands, taking a break in order to calm her jittery nerves. During the short hiatus, while she gazed about the gigantic room, she saw Cole Kendrick standing a few yards away.

She grabbed the edge of the blackjack table to steady her wobbly legs. He looked right at her, but didn't smile. Why was he here? she wondered. It was apparent he wasn't going to try to stop her. He didn't make a move to come any closer. He stood there looking at her. She wanted to run to him, to tell him she loved him and that if he could give her a little more time, she'd take him up to her room and show him just how much.

She forced herself to turn around and get back to business. Her hands trembled as she made her bet. When the dealer drew up to nineteen and stayed, she won again on twenty. Just two more good hands and she could leave.

She felt Cole's presence even before she looked up and saw him standing straight across the blackjack table from her. Their eyes met and held. Without words she pleaded with him, questioned him and then made another bet.

She won again, and her winning streak wasn't going unnoticed. A small crowd of observers had gathered around the gaming table. She looked over at Cole and saw that he was glaring at her stack of chips. She looked at him and smiled, biting on her bottom lip as the tears in the corners of her eyes threatened to fall. I love you, she told him telepathically. He smiled, and she was sure he had received her message.

Lucky continued playing blackjack, losing once and winning three more times. On her last bet, she won just a few dollars over the amount she needed. She gathered up her chips and walked away from the table while the crowd dispersed.

Lucky knew Cole was following her, but she didn't turn around. She walked to the cashier window and stood in a short line until the cashier took her chips and handed her a form through the opening in the window. After Lucky returned the form, the cashier handed her one of the copies and a check. She looked down at her winnings and laughed, pure, unadulterated, happy laughter.

She turned around and saw Cole standing a few feet away. He looked so good in his dark suit and tie, but she couldn't wait to strip him naked.

She walked over to him. "Hello, handsome."

"Hello, yourself, gorgeous."

"I'm in Atlantic City all by myself, and I'm awfully lonely." She rubbed up against the side of his arm and batted her eyelashes.

Cole couldn't keep from laughing as he continued playing her little game. "Well, I just arrived and don't have a room. My overnight bag is at the desk."

She slipped her arm around his waist, let her hand edge downward and patted his firm behind. "Let's go get your bag. I've got a room and a bed just the right size for two people."

The crowded elevator allowed Lucky and Cole to do no more than stand side by side and gaze into each other's eyes. When they reached her floor, they ran to her room, unlocked it and rushed inside. Lucky threw her arms around Cole and kissed him. He pushed her away, holding her by the shoulders.

"Wait just one minute before you ravage me," Cole said. "You're supposed to be angry with me. You should be screaming and shouting and telling me what a stupid, chauvinist jerk I am."

"All right," she said. "You're a stupid, chauvinist jerk, and I'm so glad you're here."

"Ah, Lucky." His need for her consumed him. He ached, physically and mentally, to possess her, to join their bodies and become one. His macho stupidity had hurt her, and he wanted to show her with more than words that he was sorry.

"I needed you here with me," she said.

He wanted to take her right then, just pull her down on the floor and ride the waves of their passion until he was spent. "I need you, honey. I need you so much," he whispered huskily into her ear, his tongue circling the inner crevice.

She moaned, loosening her tight grip about his body, swaying softly into him. "Cole... Cole."

His tongue moved in and out of her ear, then glided down her arched neck. When his mouth encountered the barrier of her velvet dress, he unzipped it and slowly eased the garment down her body until it fell about her ankles. Lucky raised her feet and kicked the dress aside. Cole took her by the shoulders, steadying her as his mouth moved down the front of her body.

She made soft, incoherent little sounds, almost moaning, almost crying. She wanted to touch him, but somehow she couldn't. She was too caught up in the pleasure spiraling through her own body. She felt the catch of her bra open, knew the second the round fullness of her breasts fell free and rejoiced in the feel of his big, hard hands closing over them. His first touch was gentle, tentative, but when she sighed, he squeezed, his fingers kneading the swollen mounds. Her guttural meows enticed him to torment the hard tips with his thumbs and forefingers. When his love-play reached her femininity, she arched her head, her shoulders falling backward against his arm.

"Cole... please..."

"All in good time, honey. All in good time."

Somehow his words and his actions did not seem to coincide. He reached out and ran his fingers through her hair, loosening it from the topknot, allowing it to fall freely about her shoulders. Then, quickly, carelessly, he stripped her naked. For several minutes, he didn't touch her. His eyes feasted on her nudity. He swept her into his arms and carried her to the bed.

Lucky heard a click before the soft light from the bedside lamp banished the semidarkness. The dim light cast a creamy glow across the man who was impatiently stripping the clothes from his body. Naked and aroused, Cole stood at the side of the bed, his broad chest moving in and out with the force of his labored breathing. He's all male, Lucky thought, like a big, beautiful stallion ready to mate.

Slowly Cole lowered himself onto the bed and lay down beside Lucky. He didn't touch her. He could hear her short, rapid breathing and see her silver eyes inspecting him from head to toe. He smiled, his own eyes making a thorough appraisal of her as she lay curled seductively on the beige bedspread. One arm lay across the lower part of her stomach, the other reached out for him.

He took her hand and kissed her open palm. "I'm sorry I acted like such an idiot. I had no right to forbid you to do what you thought was right."

She stared at him, her body relaxing. "I'm sorry I couldn't give in to your wishes."

"I promise I'll never try to tell you what you can or can't do."

"I won't be able to travel with you until I've paid off the mortgage. And don't offer to pay it off for me. We'll just have to have a long-distance relationship for the first year. I know it won't be ideal, but we can make it work. I promise I'll go with you to the ends of the earth if you'll just give me the chance I need—"

Cole covered her mouth with his hand, but she continued mumbling. She looked up at his smiling face and hushed immediately.

"God, woman, you talk too much. I wouldn't dream of offering to pay one dime on Holly House's mortgage. But when it's paid off, I have every intention of spending as much money on the place as I want because it's going to be my home for the rest of my life. Do you understand?" Cole dropped his hand from her mouth and clutched her shoulders as he inched his body closer and closer.

"Your home? The rest of your life?"

"I didn't take either network offer." Cole licked her shoulder, then sprinkled tiny kisses over its curved smoothness.

"You didn't?"

He continued the gentle assault, then stopped. "Turn over, honey." He nudged her gently until she complied and turned over, the back of her body facing him. "I didn't realize, until we spent those weeks apart, how much I've changed since my accident. Falling in love with you showed me what I've been missing all my life. I want you to be my wife. And I want our children to grow up in Florence at Holly House, in a small-town environment."

"You love me?"

"Yes, I love you."

"You want to marry me?"

"Yes." Cole reached down and picked up his slacks off the floor. He delved into a pocket and pulled out a small box. He extended his closed fist to her, opened his hand and flipped open the small box resting in his palm. A large, fiery gold topaz surrounded by tiny diamonds sparkled in its yellow silk bed within the box.

"Cole?"

"I love, you, Lucille Leticia Llewellyn Darnell. Will you marry me?" Cole asked, removing the ring from the jeweler's box.

"Oh, Cole. Yes, I . . . I'll marry you. I . . . I . . ."

"How about New Year's Day?"

"That soon?"

Cole reached for her left hand and lifted it to his lips for a kiss. He slipped the ring on her third finger. "I found out that I can't live without you, honey."

Lucky looked down at the ring and then up at the man she loved. "Cole, are you sure you don't want to take the sportscasting job?"

"I'm sure."

"But . . . but what will you do?"

"I'm going to coach baseball at the University of North Alabama, right there in good old Florence."

"What?"

"Well, I haven't signed the contract yet, but we're negotiating."

Lucky turned her head toward Cole. She wanted to shake the man. He'd put her through hell. But when she looked at him, her anger melted. He smiled and lay down beside her.

"Cole Kendrick, why didn't you tell me all this before I left Florence? I've been going crazy wondering how I'd exist moving from hotel to hotel. I was willing to give up everything for you, and all the while you knew I didn't have to. We're going to have to discuss this communication problem we have if we intend to have a happy—"

His hand covered her mouth again. "Have I already told you that you talk too much?"

Lucky tensed, snapping her head around quickly as she turned from him. He was right, she thought, but she'd be damned if she'd admit it to him now. Lucky moved her tongue across his palm where it rested against her mouth. He jerked his hand away.

"If you'll lay there and be quiet, I'll see what I can do about apologizing for my bad behavior," Cole told her just before his mouth touched her back, his tongue sliding slowly, sensuously downward.

"Cole?"

"Hush, woman. Can't you tell I'm trying to make love to you?"

Lucky giggled. She knew everything was going to be all right. She said a silent prayer of thanks and promised she'd never again do anything to risk losing her man. She had taken the biggest gamble of her life when she fell in love with Cole Kendrick. But she'd won, and the reward proved to be well worth the risk.

Cole looked at Lucky. She had a beautiful body, all soft and sweetly feminine from the top of her curly red hair to the bottom of her small feet. She was all woman. His woman. Lovingly he turned her over onto her stomach. While his hands moved up and down the outside line of her body, he kept remembering what it felt like to be deep inside her.

His long legs straddled her, pushing her down flat on her stomach. His tongue continued its downward trail. When his lips reached the swell of her buttocks, she groaned with pleasure. He knew she was as wild with need as he was. His tongue caressed her, leaving a hot, moist trail as it journeyed downward along her thighs to the back of her knees. While his mouth paid homage to her silky calves and feet, his hands stroked the sides of her breasts, which were pressed against the bed.

Nudging his fingers beneath their precious weight, he fondled her breasts, his thumbs grazing the turgid tips while his mouth continued to ravage her lower body. Her writhing movements inflamed him. He wanted to wait, but he couldn't. He had to take her.

"Ahh...ahh." The moan escaped his lips, filling the silent room as his manhood filled her receptive body.

The sudden, unexpected possession of her body as she lay facedown on the bed elicited primitive urges within Lucky. She moved up against the weight of his massive body as it pressed down on her lower back and legs. He moved with a wild urgency. She lifted her hips, pushing upward.

"God, woman, what are you doing?" His voice was so muffled by passion that she barely understood his words.

"Love me, Cole," she pleaded. "Love me. I don't want you to ever stop."

His lips brushed across the fiery softness of her hair, his tongue gliding down the side of her face as he thrust into her sweet body. "Turn over, honey," he said, his body driving into hers one final time before he rolled her over to face him. Her hungry eyes caressed his face and body as he hovered above her, bracing himself with his arms.

She watched his dark head descend. His mouth took hers with forceful passion, bruising its softness, his teeth nibbling at her lips. His tongue cut into the tender warmth of her mouth, stabbing again and again until she was breathless, her hands reaching out to touch his chest.

He feels so good, she thought. So marvelously hard. The thick abundance of hair beckoned her fingers, enticing her to stroke through its plushness before moving her hands down his chest to his round, shallow navel. He kissed her repeatedly as if the burning in his manhood could be transmitted to his tongue. When her hands moved below his navel, his lips abandoned her mouth to claim a tempting nipple.

"Cole!" she cried his name, her body shaking with desire.

With trembling hands, she reached out and encompassed him. He moaned deep and low.

"Yes, God, yes. Touch me, Lucky. Touch me."

"Cole, please..." She squirmed, her flushed body damp with arousal. "I want you. Please. Now."

Instead of taking her immediately as she expected, he lifted her hips, kissed her stomach and descended slowly until he reached his goal. Like a woman gone mad, Lucky clawed at his head, her knees shoving against his chest as she trembled with yearning.

"Ahh...ahh...ahh. Yes! Yes!" she screamed.

With an overpowering need possessing him, Cole lunged into her body. She mauled his broad back with her fingernails and covered his sweaty chest with feverish kisses.

The feel, the smell, the taste of him, was like a strong aphrodisiac to her senses. He felt big and hard. He smelled earthy and tasted musky sweet.

"If I'm hurting you..." Cole tried to ask her to forgive him for being so brutal in his loving.

"I want this just as much as you do."

Her admission acted as a stimulant to a man who needed no further inducement. Cole pushed into her hard and deep. In a frenzy of abandonment, they lost themselves in the joy of pleasuring each other.

While Cole moved within her, Lucky twisted and turned in ecstasy, her wet, burning body shuddering repeatedly with fulfillment. A few moments later Cole joined her, the essence of life spilling from him, filling her.

A manly growl of surrender rumbled from his chest, his body burying hers as he fell against her. "Good... good... so good."

"I love you," she whispered.

"Lucky, Lucky. What did I ever do to deserve you?"

Epilogue

———

Leticia Colette Kendrick ran down the stairs, her red pigtails bouncing up and down on her back. She raced into her mother's antique shop and crawled under a large Jacobean table.

"Lettie, what are you doing?" Lucky asked her four-year-old bundle of energy.

"Getting my ball and glove," the child replied, pushing her round little body out from under the table. She held up a child-sized baseball glove. "The guys are outside waiting for me."

Lettie dashed past her scowling mother and barely missed running into her father, who stood in the doorway.

Cole grabbed his daughter around the waist and picked her up. "Slow down, slugger. The guys aren't going anywhere. They're all waiting on the coach's daughter."

Cole looked across the room at his pregnant wife. Lucky shook her head and tried not to smile. Sometimes, at moments such as this, Cole could hardly believe his good fortune. How the hell had that trashy Kendrick kid from the streets of Memphis ever wound up married to a lady like Lucky, living in a historic mansion, with a daughter who was his spitting image, except for her red hair, and with another kid on the way?

In the five years since he and Lucky had exchanged vows in a private ceremony on New Year's Day, he'd been the happiest man alive. The love he and his wife shared grew stronger and deeper and more passionate with each passing day.

"I suppose the whole UNA baseball team is in my backyard?" Lucky asked, accustomed to Cole's players making Holly House their second home.

With Lettie squirming in his arms, Cole walked across the room and put his other arm around Lucky. "Not the whole team, honey. Just a few of the boys."

"Make sure your game stops in time for you to take Lettie to her ballet lesson at four." Lucky laid the feather duster aside and opened the lid of a traveling tea service, a recent addition to her antique shop.

"I'll get her bathed, suited up in pink leotards and at the studio in plenty of time. I promise." Cole dropped a kiss on his wife's nose.

"Me, too, Daddy," Lettie demanded, and her father gave her a quick peck.

This is the way life is meant to be, Lucky thought. She had it all. A thriving business, a lovely home, a perfectly adorable daughter and another child due to make his arrival within a month. Since she had long ago paid off the mortgage and her antique business was so successful, she and Cole had decided that at the end of the season they would close Holly House as a bed and breakfast. After all, they needed more room. Joel was living at home while he finished his senior year at UNA, Uncle Pudge still hadn't persuaded Miss Winnie to marry him and Rebecca drove down from Memphis for weekend visits almost every month.

Cole patted Lucky on her rotund belly. "This baby will probably hate baseball."

Lucky placed her hand over his where it lay on her stomach. "It would serve you right if he's wild about antiques and doesn't give a hoot for sports."

"My son?" Cole laughed. "I doubt it."

"He'll be my son, too," Lucky reminded her husband.

"He's gonna like baseball, Mommy," Lettie said. "Me and Daddy got him his own ball and glove, and a little bitty shirt with his name on it and—"

Cole put two fingers over his daughter's mouth, turned quickly and carried her toward the hallway. "You're just like your mother, Lettie. You talk too much."

Lucky smiled, remembering all the times Cole had silenced her nervous chatter with passionate kisses. She wandered around in the shop for several minutes, eyeing the feather duster from time to time, but not picking it up. Finally she walked into the hallway, through the kitchen and out the back door.

The bright springtime sunshine warmed her all over as she stood and looked out across the backyard toward the pitcher's mound. Lucky folded her arms, resting them atop her protruding stomach as she watched Cole prepare for the pitch.

Lettie gripped the small wooden bat tightly in her chubby hands as her father threw the ball. She swung. The bat made contact, and the ball sailed through the air. The seven young men in the field cheered as Lettie raced to first base.

"That'a way to go, Lettie!" Lucky yelled.

Cole's dark eyes rested on his beautiful wife while she shouted their daughter's praises. Lucky turned, smiling at him, and they exchanged loving glances, their eyes saying everything. In that one moment, they shared remembered pleasures, promises for future dreams and thanks for their present happiness.

*   *   *   *   *

Available now from

SILHOUETTE® Desire™

MAN OF THE MONTH 1991

What's a hero? He's a man who's...

Handsome	Charming
Intelligent	Dangerous
Rugged	Enigmatic
Lovable	Adventurous
Tempting	Hot-blooded
Undoubtedly sexy	Irresistible

He's everything you want—and he's back! Twelve brand-new MAN OF THE MONTH heroes from twelve of your favorite authors...

NELSON'S BRAND by Diana Palmer	in January
OUTLAW by Elizabeth Lowell	in February
MCALLISTER'S LADY by Naomi Horton	in March
THE DRIFTER by Joyce Thies	in April
SWEET ON JESSIE by Jackie Merritt	in May
THE GOODBYE CHILD by Ann Major	in June

And that's just the beginning! So no matter what time of year, no matter what season, there's a dynamite MAN OF THE MONTH waiting for you...*only* in Silhouette Desire.

SILHOUETTE·INTIMATE·MOMENTS®

NORA ROBERTS
Night Shadow

People all over the city of Urbana were asking, Who was that masked man?

Assistant district attorney Deborah O'Roarke was the first to learn his secret identity . . . and her life would never be the same.

The stories of the lives and loves of the O'Roarke sisters began in January 1991 with NIGHT SHIFT, Silhouette Intimate Moments #365. And if you want to know more about Deborah and the man behind the mask, look for NIGHT SHADOW, Silhouette Intimate Moments #373.

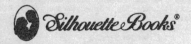

Silhouette Books®